married to a Stranger

Nahid Rachlin

City Lights　　**San Francisco**

MARRIED TO A STRANGER

© 1983 by Nahid Rachlin
First published by E.P. Dutton, Inc.
First City Lights Books edition 1993.
All Rights Reserved

Cover design: Rex Ray

Excerpt from Forugh Farrokhzad, "The Wind-Up Doll," in *An Anthology of Modern Persian Poetry*, translated by Ahmad Karimi-Hakkak, Westview Press, 1978. Reprinted by permission of Ehsan Yarshater, General Editor of Bibliotheca Persica.

Library of Congress Cataloging in Publication Data

Rachlin, Nahid.
  Married to a stranger.
  I. Title.
PS3568.A2443M 1983 813'.54 83-1461
ISBN: 0-87286-276-3 (pbk)

City Lights Books are available to bookstores through our primary distributor: Subterranean Company. P. O. Box 160, 265 S. 5th St., Monroe, OR 97456. 503-847-5274. Toll-free orders 800-274-7826. FAX 503-847-6018. Our books are also available through library jobbers and regional distributors. For personal orders and catalogs, please write to City Lights Books, 261 Columbus Avenue, San Francisco CA 94133.

CITY LIGHTS BOOKS are edited by Lawrence Ferlinghetti and Nancy J. Peters and published at the City Lights Bookstore, 261 Columbus Avenue, San Francisco, CA 94133.

For Howard and Leila

Minou stood in front of the partly fogged up mirror in the public baths, looking at herself, smiling at her own reflection—brown hair, now black from being wet, brown eyes, an olive skin. It was early morning and pale light flowed in from windows near the ceiling. In different places in the vast room other women sat in clusters by pans of water. Except for a red cloth that each wore around her hips, everyone was naked.

The following day Minou was going to be married to Javad Partovi. Sparks of excitement leaped out of her as she thought of that. How could it be that she would be married to him, living with him forever, day after day, when he had been unattainable, no more than a fantasy, only a short while ago? Her future had been amorphous, a stretch of undefined days.

In a matter of weeks everything had changed. She would be called Minou Partovi, no longer Minou Hakimi. She and Javad together would leave Ahvāz, where she had lived all her life.

She walked away from the mirror, now all fogged up, to the center of the room, where her two aunts sat waiting. "Remember not to act eager the first night," Aunt Narghes said as soon as Minou sat down. "Let him believe you're shy. It's better for you to wait a night or two before giving in."

Minou nodded, uncomfortable with the conversation.

"It's going to hurt and bleed," Mehri said.

"It's like dying," Narghes said.

More women were coming in, the red cloths around them like heaps of roses, their voices humming like bees.

"I remember my own wedding bath," Narghes went on, dipping a rough cloth into the pan and scrubbing Minou's arms. Narghes' gold, leaf-shaped necklace was lusterless in the shadow of her neck. Her long, thin breasts trembled on her stomach as she moved to and fro. "I soaked myself the whole day and washed and washed. It used to be different in those days, another Iran. Everyone brought lunch and sat in the baths all day long, letting the henna take on a deep color. Now people come in and rush out in a couple of hours."

"Of course it's different now," Minou said. "It's so many years since you got married."

Narghes moved behind Minou to wash her back. "It's good to get rid of the old skin."

"We started to get ready for our wedding when we were less than ten years old," Mehri said. "We sat together, eating watermelon seeds and sewing and embroidering things for our dowry. On warm days we sat in our shady courtyard or on the roof. In the winter we stayed in the living room with the fire always burning."

"I was the first to be married. I showed my sisters everything," Narghes said.

"Narghes was the prettiest of the three of us with those large dark eyes and hair full of ringlets, and the most proud," Mehri said, rubbing her own heels with a porous stone. "Your mother was the liveliest. She bounced around and laughed a lot. She had white chubby hands with dimples at her knuckles." She smiled. "I had the best disposition."

"We cried before we got married. None of us were happy with our parents' choices. We begged them not to force us into it. Finally we gave in. You're lucky your father is letting you marry someone of your own choosing."

"He was afraid I wouldn't marry anyone else." Minou was still incredulous herself that he had consented.

Several women came in and sat very close to them.

"This is the second time she had a miscarriage," one of the women said. "The doctor said maybe she will never be able to carry the full nine months."

"You look pregnant. God bless it, is it your eighth?"

"Yes. I don't know how I'm going to manage."

"The God who puts the baby in your belly will provide for him."

"I'm so tired, I thought I'd abort this one."

"That's like killing. The fetus has a soul from the beginning."

"It was just a passing thought."

"One good thing about being finished with having children is that your husband doesn't expect you to lie with him. He has no excuse to force you into it."

"My husband tries anyway. Nothing stops him."

"Poor Narghes suffered so much for not having children." Mehri's voice reached Minou above the others. "She did everything possible to get pregnant. She lit candles at shrines, gave prayer sessions, alms to the poor.

3

She saw doctors and fortunetellers, but nothing worked."

"And I've always loved children," Narghes said.

"Sometimes God's will is incomprehensible to us," Mehri said.

"It could have been bad for you to give birth to a baby," Minou said by way of consolation.

"You get married and trouble starts." Narghes shook her head in resignation. "In addition to my own misery I had to put up with Hossein's anger and grief. He brought in a *sigheh* over me, hoping she would bear a child for him, but she didn't have any better luck than I did."

"It doesn't matter if you're happy or unhappy, rich or poor, on this earth. We're all stripped to the minimum on the Day of Judgment, when we have to answer for our-selves before God," Mehri remarked.

But Narghes went on, "Hossein would come home at lunchtime and the two of them went into her room. I couldn't drown out their voices even though they kept the door shut. I still remember her face, white as a china doll's." She turned to Minou. "I hope you won't be childless."

"That's far into the future," Minou said.

"The only joy I've had since I got married has been the children," Mehri said.

Minou thought of the exuberance that came over Mehri's household when she was about to give birth to a child and afterward when she had the baby. Lanterns were hung on trees, making their courtyard extraordinarily bright at night. Laughter poured out from behind shut doors. Then that mood flickered out and the family became a bundle of concerns of various kinds. Still there was a gaiety in Mehri that Narghes lacked, as if Mehri had somehow gotten a better flow of life than her sister.

Narghes got up. "I want to get some fresh air. I'll bring

back the *sharbat*." She went toward the curtained opening leading to the dressing room.

Mehri began carefully putting henna, which she had mixed with water, on the strands of her hair. Reddish water ran down her temples as she matted down the henna.

One of the women sitting nearby pointed to Minou and whispered to another woman, "She's getting married."

Several women turned around and scrutinized Minou. Then they began to whisper among themselves.

Narghes came back, carrying a tray with the *sharbat* glasses on it. She served the cardamom-scented drink to the women around them. One of the women opened a bottle of rose water and splashed drops of it on everyone. The air was filled with its fragrance. The somber conversation was momentarily replaced by a gayer one of blessing the wedding.

Then an old woman said, loudly, "Look at her, she's brought such a big boy with her." A boy about seven years old was bouncing up and down on his mother's lap, tug-·ging at her ample breasts.

"Shame," another woman said, putting henna on her nails.

"They should make stricter rules," the old woman said.

"Yes, they're getting lax in every respect."

A tall, lanky woman came in and sat not far from Minou. Her expression was restrained, and Minou noticed that attached to her white and flaccid arm were three large leeches, swollen and deep red.

"I have bad blood," she explained, noticing Minou's stare. "They suck the blood until they're bloated and then they fall off."

"I see," Minou said, nauseous at the sight.

"Ah," the woman groaned, closing her eyes.

The place was becoming hectic with different threads of conversation running together, children getting tired and impatient and kicking against the wet ground, splashing water at one another. Faces were flushed, voices a little shrill.

Mehri leaned over Minou and whispered, "Don't forget the pubic hair. It's time to get rid of it." She put a greenish substance in a bowl and mixed it with water. "Take some of this and put it on it."

Minou got up and went to one of the shower rooms, carrying the bowl with her. She put the greenish substance on her pubic hair and waited. In a few moments she plucked the hair, which came off easily. She turned on the shower and stood under it for a long time. She touched her breasts, her thighs. Her breasts were small and firm, her thighs slender.

The gentle ripple of water, the solitude, began to calm her, making her aunts' warnings recede. She thought of the room that she and Javad would furnish with her dowry—a satin-covered bed, gauze curtains through which she would see flowering trees. She would lie beside Javad at night and tell him the events of the day. He would hold her head on his chest, caress her.

Nothing else mattered at the moment beyond the urgency she felt in her flesh to unite with him.

She had met Javad Partovi less than six months before, a few weeks before the end of the term. It was 1975. She was eighteen, in the last year of high school. The day was unusually balmy, with pollen floating in the air. The seed heads of dandelions dangled outside of the window. The classroom vibrated with the loud, confused voices of adolescent girls. Minou looked down at her composition book, outlining with a pencil the titles of the chapters, making a snake, a donkey, or a tree.

The door opened and the principal, a tall, heavy woman, walked in, accompanied by a man other than the usual composition teacher. Everyone looked up and then sat down, sinking into fearful silence. The principal was quick to anger and harsh in her punishments.

"This is Mr. Partovi. He'll be teaching you for the rest of the year," she said.

Mr. Partovi smiled at the class, reticently. He looked to be in his early thirties, was thin and tall, and wore glasses. His clothes were well cut but casual, a green corduroy suit and a beige shirt. He looked serious and yet had an aura of great gentleness. Minou thought he reminded her of someone, but no specific person came to her mind. He looked a little like other intellectual men—writers, poets, revolutionaries—whose photographs she had seen in magazines and newspapers.

"Mr. Meli has left for personal reasons," the principal went on, "and won't be back until next year."

Minou stared at Javad Partovi, drawn to him instantly—it was his smile, something meditative about his eyes, a lurking sadness.

"Well, the class is yours," the principal said to him.

She left and he began to talk. He told them that he had been teaching in Abadan and came here because he needed a change of scene. He asked them which authors they had been reading and told them his own favorite was Sadeq Hedayat, a young Iranian writer who wrote surrealistic stories and who had committed suicide in France. He said he translated short stories from English into Persian. He mentioned a few that had appeared in *Setareh*, a monthly magazine, and asked the class if they had read any of them. Minou subscribed to the magazine and read it cover to cover as soon as it arrived at her house. She was excited by his passionate interest in literature. The approach of the previous teacher had been dull, with emphasis on grammar and formal structure.

He went on to say that he hoped everyone would participate in class discussion, that he considered their comments as important as his own.

8

The bell rang and Javad Partovi left immediately. He seemed to be in a hurry. The others began to leave also.

The courtyard was filled with students standing in clusters before doorways and by palm trees, talking, giggling. Some walked across the yard in pairs, their hands clasped together. Minou dashed to the washroom to see if she could find Farzin, her best friend, who had left the class before her. The washroom was noisy with various threads of conversation.

"I'm never going to be happy, never."

"We live in prison here."

"I heard about something awful. Remember that tall, strange-looking girl living near our house? She drowned in their pool last night. She had an epileptic fit when no one was home and fell into the pool. Her mother found her when she came home. She ran out into the street screaming, 'She's dead, my daughter is dead.'"

"Oh no."

"Did you hear about that suicide in the boys' school? A boy in his senior year shot himself. He left a note that he couldn't go on living."

"Yes, he was that handsome, very serious-looking boy."

"My menstrual period was so heavy, I'm still a little weak from it. Blood kept coming out in huge, thick clots for so long I thought it would never stop."

Farzin was standing by the mirror, washing a smudge of ink from her face. Minou joined her.

"What did you think of the new teacher?" she asked.

"He's a fresh voice."

"There's something different about him. He's so gentle, not authoritarian." The difference was a signal to Minou of another world, the world of foreign movies and foreign books.

9

The bell rang again, announcing the end of the ten-minute break.

Going home that afternoon, Minou kept thinking about him. Every word he said had penetrated deeply. She wished she were still in the class, listening to his voice with its gentle rise and fall. There was an odd, injured look about him, a wound not far beneath the surface of his self-confident manner. She imagined him pacing his office or the hall absentmindedly as if looking for something he had lost but not sure precisely where to look for it. He would pause and put his hand on his temple, thinking, or would touch the wall meaninglessly.

The streets were noisy with traffic. The air smelled of fish and petroleum. The sounds of children chasing one another in and out of alleys and doorways, cars, horsecarts, vendors advertising their merchandise, music blaring out of shops and movie houses, hammers banging on metal in the blacksmiths' bazaar, mewing of stray cats, fused and whirled around in her head.

She saw her own image floating on the windowpanes of the shops, a small, pretty girl.

She slowed down when she approached Pahlavi Street, onto which the balcony surrounding the upper floor of their house protruded. At the cinema across from their house a man was changing the billboard that displayed photographs of Barbra Streisand and Omar Sharif in an embrace, of them staring into each other's face, their eyes love-struck. The movie was *Funny Girl*. A line had already formed for the first show. Most of the men wore dark sunglasses, the women white shoes.

At her house she paused by the twin doors and listened. She hoped no one would be home so that she could go to her room directly without her mother or father complaining that perhaps her school uniform was a little too short, or wasn't she a little late coming home? She could hear a flow of talk from her father's law office on the second floor. He saw several clients every day, sometimes into the evening. They talked about the possibilities of getting out of a long jail sentence, protecting a piece of property from being taken over by someone, how to find a runaway husband. Some of the clients were well dressed and fashionable—a woman, for instance, who wore a low-cut black blouse and a short skirt and kept crossing and recrossing her long, stockinged legs. Some looked destitute. Her father said he took them on as a charitable act and did not expect to be paid by them. There were unpleasant scenes sometimes—an old man weeping and climbing down the back stairway and her father shouting at him, "Why do you bring that kind of problem to me?" or a man refusing to leave until her father made Ali, their servant, drag him away.

She took the door leading into the courtyard. The palm trees, clusters of dates hanging from them, stood very still around flower beds. Fish floated slowly and lazily in the pool.

In her room she found a letter on her desk from Sohrab, her brother, who was studying in the United States. She opened it quickly. There was a photograph enclosed in it, of him with a young woman. The two of them were sitting on a park bench, holding hands and smiling into the camera. Several tall buildings stood beyond the park.

". . . It has been snowing here for days. I look out of the window and see whiteness everywhere. The sounds of traffic, of footsteps, are muffled. People on the street, the few you see, are huddled in layers of clothes. It amazes me how quiet the streets are. Nothing seems to happen here, but I like the silence. I've met at least one worthwhile person. I'm enclosing her picture. . . ."

Minou kept dwelling on the snow and the pretty woman

who held Sohrab's hand so naturally, as if she were his sister or happily married to him. She imagined herself standing on that street with snowflakes falling on her hair and face. She had seen snow on the top of the mountains outside of Ahvāz, whiteness capping the rugged blackness. Once on the way to school she had seen the rain change into icicles, pieces of ice hitting the windows, the ground, sounding like drums beating. She had held her head up, letting her face be bombarded by them.

Many times she had asked her parents to send her to the United States when she finished high school, but she always lost the argument. Her father said, "It's out of the question. A young girl alone is asking for trouble." Minou said, "I could go to the same university as Sohrab, or one near him. Then I won't be alone." He snapped, "Sohrab has work to do. He won't be able to follow you around to make sure you stay out of trouble."

She put down the letter and the photograph and started to do homework, but loud traffic noises intruded. Through the window she could see the dentist across the street working on a patient, who sat passively in a plush chair. The dentist, a young, handsome man, kept moving back and forth between the patient's mouth and his instruments. Suddenly a sermon from the loudspeaker in a nearby mosque filled the air.

"A woman who is guilty of lewdness before or after marriage ought to be confined to the house until death takes her. A man who gives in to temptation should be punished as well. As believers, we should be prepared for severe penalties." The *aghound's* voice rose to a higher pitch. "Every time you're tempted to indulge in sin of any kind, imagine yourself burning perpetually in the depths of hell with fire around you and boiling water poured into your throat. On the other hand, if you're good on this earth the

Garden of Eden awaits you, where you will recline on thrones, trees bearing fruit will bow to you, rivers will flow underneath you, rivers of unpolluted water, of milk that will not spoil, of wine, of clear honey. Drinks will be brought to you by private servants, served to you in goblets of gold and silver. You will be dressed in robes of finest silk, embroidered with gold. There will be no idle talk there, but murmurs of 'peace, peace.' The air will be neither hot nor bitter cold. There will be food to your liking anytime of the day. All this instead of the fires of hell. Yes, hell is a dungeon for those who don't obey, where men and women moan and beg, a little too late, for forgiveness, where human flesh falls off...."

She got up and shut the window but the *aghound*'s voice still penetrated.

Since Sohrab left she had become restless. The town of Ahvāz seemed to have shrunk. She was stifled by the house they lived in. There was a numbing effect from the whirring of the ceiling fans, all the rugs, some piled on top of one another in each room, the heavy, shellacked furniture. So many empty rooms and useless hallways. Dead flies fallen on the floor or caught in the sticky paper Ali hung on ceilings, tepid water in the large pool in the courtyard, with the fish sucking in the oxygen laboriously. The air filled with the odor of petroleum from the nearby oil pipes.

She could not bear her mother's fretfulness—her mother seemed burdened by an incurable unhappiness that made her voice ring with perpetual annoyance. She constantly picked on Ali.

"Why do you just sit there and stare at the pigeons? Can't you get up and do something useful—dust the furniture or sweep the courtyard?"

Ali kept sitting there.

"Don't you hear me? Do you want me to tell Homayoon *khan* that you sit there all day and stare at the pigeons?"

The mention of Minou's father's name made Ali get up immediately.

She criticized Ali in a muttering way: "Oh, you bought the fish from that store again. I told you not to, his fish aren't as fresh as the ones from the store on the corner. Next time don't put so much water in the rice, it comes out mushy."

Ali shook his head vaguely, squinting at the sky, not really listening.

Minou could not bear her father's controlling presence. He was difficult to please. The turmeric had to be just right in the *khoresh*, the meat cooked to an exact degree, or else he would push his plate away. On Fridays, when he kept his office shut, he listened to the news every hour on the huge radio in the living room. He turned the volume high so that it could be heard in any part of the house. ". . . Iran has donated one hundred million *tomans* from oil revenues toward the relief of the famine in Africa. . . . Iran sold three million barrels of oil to the United States at a slightly raised price of eighty-five *tomans* per barrel. In a meeting with OPEC nations, a new price was set for oil, with Iran leading the discussion. . . ."

Highly affected by what he heard, he paced the room or came over to Minou, saying, "Didn't I tell you that we're a powerful nation?" He spoke to her in a teacher-like manner. "In ancient times Iran shone like a jewel among all nations. We sent a chill down the Greeks' spines, surpassed Rome in every respect. We were known throughout the world for our intelligence and culture. We had the best poets, great musicians, philosophers. . . ."

He disapproved of whatever he construed as "communistic," such as compulsory education. He lived in terror of communism. He tore up *Mother* by Maxim Gorky, which he found in Minou's room, because it was by a communist Russian author. He told her to stay away from such propagandist books. He was pro-Shah with reservations about the weakness of the Shah's character, which allowed those around him to commit criminal acts in his name.

The sight of the empty rooms that had belonged to Sohrab and to her grandmother, now dead, depressed Minou. Her grandmother had lived in Aunt Narghes' house but spent several weeks a year in her other daughters' houses. She sat in one spot for long periods of time. "My legs feel hollow, all my bones do. I'm like a hollow tin box," she said. She liked the sun. She said her legs always felt as if they had ice filling their empty spaces. When the sun was out, she piled up blankets on her legs while she fanned her face with a hand fan as if the two parts of her body were in different temperature zones. She liked to mend the clothes Minou's mother collected into a pile. She gave the empty thread spools to Minou and told her to string them together and make a necklace. Sometimes she did the ironing. The heavy metal iron was heated by coals inside it. It gave out sparks, occasionally scorching the fabric. She cursed the iron when that happened. Then she folded and piled the clothes neatly with the seams in one straight line.

In the afternoon they all gathered around a samovar and had tea. Her grandmother liked her tea strong and drank it slowly through a piece of rock sugar held between her front teeth. The color of her tea exactly matched the amber ring she always wore on her forefinger. She measured the tea to get that shade—two thirds of the glass from the teapot and one third hot water from the samovar. She liked exactness in everything (when she peeled apples, she took the skin off in a long, narrow strip, and then cut them into eight pieces, a perfection she had reached over the years), a defense against the chaos of all the children and grandchildren, births and deaths around her, against the unpredictability of fate—that Narghes had borne no children, that one of her own children had died in infancy. She said, with fresh grief in her voice, "I used to fill up a tub with water and let her play in it. Sometimes I splashed water on the ground and she would giggle and crawl from one puddle to another. It was so easy to make her laugh. And then she died. It was hard to believe so much life would end." Looking skyward, she said, "But of course she's there in heaven."

At night she spread her bed in the open hall that connected the two clusters of rooms on the second floor. She sat there from early evening on and read the Koran, the pages of which had yellow stains on them from turmeric and saffron. She ran her rosary between her fingers and whispered litanies to God's greatness and beneficence. Then she lay down and went to sleep, her body limp under the *chador* that she kept on her instead of a sheet. Sometimes Minou slept on a mattress next to her and woke at dawn to her praying, reclining and rising on a black and white cloth.

She had lived through so much, such as the time Reza Shah forced all the women to take off their *chadors*—the soldiers would literally pull them off their heads if they were caught wearing them on the street. The women began to wear kerchiefs when they went out. Thank God that did not last for too long.

She addressed her granddaughter as "dear Minou." She took Minou's temperature at the slightest complaint, made her lie in bed, and fed her soup. Once Minou was running around the courtyard with a twig in her hand. She fell, and the stick went into the roof of her mouth, injuring it. Minou started to cry. Her mother said, "Stop crying, it's nothing." But her grandmother put her on her lap and looked inside her mouth. "It looks red, it must hurt." She rocked Minou on her lap until she calmed down. Then she said, "You shouldn't run around so much, you aren't a boy. You ought to sit down and do some sewing and cooking. Don't imitate your brother. A boy can do anything he wants, but a girl..."

If Minou had a fight with Sohrab, her grandmother automatically came to her defense. "Minou's right," she would say before hearing both sides. She hardly paid any attention to Sobrab. She gave Minou delicacies she kept in a little sack. She told Minou not to tell Sohrab about it.

Minou's grandmother constantly warned her against men. She told Minou the story of a man who used to stand in doorways on dark, empty streets when she herself was a young girl, and jump out when he saw a girl passing by. He would force the girl into a car and take her away to the desert and do bad things to her. If she resisted he would cut her up and put her limbs in a pail, covered by a cloth. He carried the pail everywhere with him. He was caught when someone spotted blood on the cloth. He would be dead or rotting in jail now, but there were men like him everywhere.

Once she gave Minou a rag doll with braided black hair and blue-black eyes, wearing a full embroidered dress. She had made the doll herself, and it smelled of camphor from lying in a trunk for years. Minou took it with her everywhere. Once, going to a doctor with her mother to have her tonsils taken out, Minou left it on the bus. For days she expected it to turn up in her room or behind the door, found miraculously by someone and brought over.

Not long after her grandmother died, Sohrab left for the United States. Minou missed him as she did her grandmother. When they were children he had taken her on long walks. They went inside vacant garages and dim hallways of houses. They explored the road stretching along the river with oil pipes cutting across it, the hot desert beyond the road, a little frightened by the awesome monotony of the sand dunes. They went through quiet fields and dug out watermelons and lettuce. There was no end to these explorations. Finally they dragged themselves home, exhausted, their clothes soiled with dirt, perhaps a sleeve torn. Their mother would scream at them: this was no way to behave, to disappear for hours and to come home looking the way they did. Were they not afraid of their father's punishment? She made them change their clothes and take turns washing themselves in the shower room installed in the corner of the courtyard. Sometimes they bribed their mother by bringing back flowers and fruit for her.

Once, on an unfamiliar street, they were attacked by a group of boys. After a brief, awkward fight they ran away, Minou with her nose bleeding and bruises on her arm. Her father forbade her to go out for a week. Another time they got lost and a policemen took them to the police station and they had to wait there in terror until their father arrived to take them back. This time he forbade both of them to go any farther than a few blocks from their house for a month.

In the afternoon, when everyone took naps, Minou used to tiptoe into Sohrab's room, and they talked in low tones.

Sohrab teased her that she was not his real sister, that he found her one day on the riverbank inside a watermelon. The watermelon rolled out of the river and began to spin around and around on the sand like a pinwheel, crashed against a rock, and broke open. Then he saw an infant inside one of the halves. He leaned over and picked up the infant. It was naked and he could see that it was a girl. He wrapped her wet body in his jacket and put her in the basket of his bicycle. At home he begged his parents to take her. They refused at first because who would want a girl? Then they took her in as they would a stray cat.

As Sohrab and Minou grew older they became more daring. They wandered in the vicinity of the nightclub. The nightclub, always filled with male customers, had live entertainment—pretty belly dancers and singers. Behind the club there was a brothel. A fat, heavily made up woman in bright clothes always sat on the steps of the two-story building. Other similarly dressed women looked out of its windows. Some of the windows had pieces of cloth nailed to them. Loud music flowed from the building. Sleazy-looking men with oily, styled hair went in and out of the house or stood on the sidewalk watching. The women smiled, winked, beckoned to them with their fingers.

Minou had seen a woman lying on the sidewalk of that street, her body jerking up and down. She had sores on her lips and her hair was missing in patches. Sohrab said, "She's a prostitute. She has a venereal disease, syphilis probably. She can go bald and blind from it. No one would want to go near her now."

On the same street she found a white, wrinkled balloon on the ground. Sohrab made her drop it. "That's not a balloon, that's something..." He whispered in her ear, "Something that men use when they sleep with women."

What he said sounded strange, a little frightening.

Once, vacationing in the country with their parents, she and Sohrab watched, through trees, a man and a woman making love under a mosquito net. They were well into the woods and surrounded by foliage. But the moon shone brightly on them and Minou could see the silhouettes of their bodies, twisting and curling in a mysterious dance. She could hear their gay spurts of laughter. She felt Sohrab's hand moving, distractedly, up and down her arm. In the same distracted manner he caressed the back of her neck. She drew away gently. After a while they walked away. They did not mention what they had seen, suddenly shy with one another.

Then Sohrab began to stay out late at night. Their father called him to his office. Minou stood behind the door and listened.

"Don't ever let me catch you with a girl again. Do you know the price I will have to pay if her parents find out about it, if you get her..." He added softly but audibly, "pregnant."

Sohrab muttered, "I'm not a child anymore."

Their father said, softly again, "If you need a woman you come with me to the nightclub."

Minou could not hear the rest of the conversation.

Now Sohrab was far away and had all the freedom he wanted while Minou was left here in Ahvāz.

"The girl was no more than twelve but her eyes looked around her with the weariness of an old woman. She was combing her long, black hair. The mother arranged it into a smooth, lank mass and adorned it with bright silver stars. Then she gave her a long velveteen dress and jewels to wear.

"'Where are we going, Mother?' the girl asked.

"'To the bazaar,' the mother said absently and made the girl get up and turn around to make sure everything in her grooming was right.

"They went to the square and got on a horsecart. The horsecart moved slowly through the crowded streets.

"At the edge of the bazaar the mother got out and the girl followed her. The bazaar was very old. Its ceiling was covered with black cloth and on its walls hung withered flowers and golden yarn. Heavy perfume and incense barely masked the musty smell in the air. Men, wearing thread-bare turbans and long garments, were standing by shop doors, calling people to buy their merchandise. They had bloodshot eyes and greedily pursed lips.

"'Look inside, you'll find what you're here for,' one of them said raucously.

"'Go in and you won't regret it,' said another, 'you whose pockets jingle with gold.'

"'We have all sizes, all colors,' shouted the third, raising his voice above the others.

"Men and women of all ages walked about slowly, looking inside the dim shops, whispering things.

"'Take me back, Mother, this place frightens me,' the girl said. What she had seen in the dim stores was girls dressed in elaborate clothes and jewelry, like herself, sitting on tall stools, their hands bound behind them.

"'Go on,' the mother said, prodding her forward.

"Then the mother stopped by a shop in the center of the bazaar, where a thick column of sun came in through a crack in the ceiling.

"An old man wearing a grayish turban and suit was standing in the doorway of the shop, staring into space.

"'Here's the girl I told you about,' the mother said, stepping closer to the man. 'Isn't she pretty?'

"The man turned his eyes slowly to the girl.

"'Not bad, but maybe a bit underdeveloped,' he said. Then he began to laugh, revealing crooked yellow teeth.

"The girl began to tremble but remained silent. The man put his hand on her back and led her inside.

"'Sit on that stool and cross your legs.' He took down a long pink cloth from a rafter. 'I'm going to tie your hands behind you—don't worry, I'll be gentle.'

"The girl sat on the stool and watched her mother walk away while the man bound her hands. Men began to come in one by one or in twos and looked her over.

"The girl screamed for her mother, but there was no sign of her. She was doomed, she knew, with the other girls."

Minou stopped reading and waited for reactions. The room swayed before her.

She had written the composition late at night, when she could shut the door to her room without her mother, father, or Ali coming in and inquiring why she did not sit outside on the veranda and do her schoolwork in the fresh air, why she was working so hard. Then she had put the pages inside her schoolbag so that no one would see them on her desk and read them. The idea had come to her suddenly like a spontaneous but frightening song. Once it came, she wrote the story quickly from the beginning to the end, with very few changes.

Now she intensely wanted Javad Partovi's approval. What did his silence mean? What if he did not like it or was even contemptuous of the idea behind it? Her attraction to him was so sudden and blind that it felt like a natural catastrophe, a thunderstorm, a flood.

"Well," Javad Partovi said to the class, "what are your reactions?"

"It's very interesting," Farzin said. "It's unusual." She glanced at Minou.

"It sounds unreal," Mahvash said. "I like some things in it."

"It's well written but unreal," Soroor remarked.

Javad Partovi looked at his watch. He said, "A girl bound and sold, a powerful metaphor. It's a refreshing piece."

"Thank you." Minou was blushing, she knew.

"You could expand it a bit, make it into a longer story."

"I'll try."

The bell rang. He asked everyone to give him their compositions, even those who had read. Minou left hers on his desk and lingered for a moment. She wished she could stay on and ask more questions. It seemed to her that Javad

24

Partovi would understand her totally. But he was surrounded by several other students, handing in their compositions and talking with him.

She walked out, floating. She was full of an energy that made it hard for her to stand still.

When she got home that afternoon, her mother was having tea in the living room with her friend Shamsi. From the hallway Minou could hear them complaining about the way butchers cheated their customers, how hard it was to find good servants these days, the noise and dust, how they got headaches from it all and had constantly to take aspirins.

Shamsi visited Minou's mother frequently. She came over in the morning and did not leave until late afternoon. They would sit in chairs for a while. Then, getting tired, they would sit on the rug with their legs stretched out in front of them and drink glass after glass of tea and talk.

"Come in," her mother said to Minou.

Minou stood in the doorway, eager to go to her room. One wall was covered by blown-up photographs of Sohrab and of herself, another wall with two large framed cloths with pictures of cats that her mother had embroidered on them.

"I have to go to my room. I have a lot of work."

"I haven't seen you for a long time," Shamsi said.

"She's always studying," her mother replied for her.

"What for? You're going to be diapering babies anyway. Too much studying is no good for you. It will hurt your eyes and make you age faster."

Minou shrugged, slightly intimidated. Shamsi had the bearing of a career woman even though she was a rich doctor's wife and spent her days mostly visiting her friends. She had plucked her eyebrows to an arch. She chain-smoked. She was quick and shrewd, a contrast to Minou's mother, who was soft-spoken, a little helpless-looking.

"She knows nothing of housework," her mother said. "She can't even cook rice."

"That's how schoolgirls are these days. But you ought to learn soon, that's what's going to matter when you get married, not whether you know the laws of chemistry."

"She needs some practical sense," Minou's mother remarked.

"When is Sohrab going to be finished with school?" Shamsi asked Minou's mother.

"Not for a few years. He wants to go on and get his doctorate."

"That's just like him. He's been like that all his life, studious. But before you know it he will be finished and back home."

From a radio Ali turned on, music flowed into the room, a popular song: "I'm enslaved to your love, please don't let me die from it, my heart is already half-broken. Your pearl teeth, your wine-colored hair, your eyes mysterious as the night sky..."

Minou walked away. Shamsi's and her mother's voices followed her.

"She has refused so many suitors," her mother said.

"I want to marry both of my daughters as soon as possible. That would be a big burden off my back."

"It's so hard to raise girls."

Minou went into her room, forlorn at the thought of spending her life with a man forced on her by her parents. She would guard herself against the man, keeping a kernel inside herself in which she would hide everything important. Her last suitor had been a lawyer, not much younger than her father. He had smooth, ink-black hair and black eyes and had worn a suit and a tie. Looking at him had made her giggle nervously. Later she cried and begged her parents not to marry her off to him. Finally they conceded, but sooner or later they would try to force someone else on her. They would not listen to her pleas indefinitely. The thought that Javad Partovi might turn out to be her next suitor had never entered her mind, not even as a fantasy. Even in her imagination she could go only as far as having a private conversation with him, telling him she had never liked a teacher as much as him.

5

On a late afternoon Minou and her mother were sitting on the rug in the living room, talking. The armchairs and the sofa, of heavy dark wood with wine-colored velveteen covers, stood behind them uselessly. A pile of magazines, filled mostly with recipes, light humor, and gossip about famous people, lay on the floor next to her mother, who had been looking through them when Minou came in.

"What am I going to do with myself when school ends?"

"You will get married, what else?" Her mother lay down. "My back aches from all the worrying I do."

Her mother rarely listened to her; she was so preoccupied by her own daily burdens. A fuzzy mist seemed to surround her, blurring her vision.

"Your father has been staying out late again. It was nearly dawn when he returned last night."

"You ought to try to stop him."

"Impossible. He thinks it's his privilege to do what he wants."

The stray yellow cat that Ali fed regularly on the porch came in, swishing its tail. Then it wandered back outside.

"You could try a little harder." It was humiliating, his will always dominating theirs.

"I know there's no point."

"Shirin, Shirin," her father called to her mother from his office.

Her mother got up promptly and started to walk toward the office.

In a moment Minou could hear their voices rising and falling without being able to distinguish the words. They seemed to be arguing about something. Then she was able to hear some of what they said.

"It's lonely for me," her mother said.

"I need refreshment at night."

"You could take me instead of going to that club full of...whores."

They stopped talking. She thought she heard her mother crying.

Minou continued sitting there. Had her father ever loved her mother? When he went out in the evening he took particular care with his clothes, making sure his shoes were shined, his suit ironed, his tie knotted perfectly. He neatly parted his hair halfway to the side and smoothed it down. She shuddered at the thought of his going to a prostitute. A girl in her high school was completely bald and wore a wig. Once the wig had blown away with the wind and exposed her shiny, hairless head. She had run after the wig, crying. There were rumors that the girl's father had a venereal disease and had transmitted it to her. The year before, passing her father's office, Minou had inadvertently come across a sight that shocked her. Through the door's narrow opening she saw her father and Khadijeh, the young maid who worked for them, lying naked on the rug. He was rubbing his hand on her buttocks and on the hump of her back, a deformity that had been with her since birth and gave her a slightly grotesque look in spite of her pretty face. Minou was frozen to the spot. Her father kept kissing and caressing Khadijeh. Then he stood up, exposing his penis. Khadijeh got to her knees and reached for the penis with her mouth. Minou drew back, as if someone had slapped her. She had thought the act of lovemaking would be surrounded by a mysterious glow, full of sparks, fading into darkness and rising again. If there was a texture to it, it would be translucent like a thin, gauzy fabric. She was not prepared for this full nakedness, this grossness. She never told anyone what she had seen, but it came back to her like a hallucination. For a while there was talk of marrying Ali to Khadijeh. They often sat together on the terrace and talked. Finally Khadijeh gave her answer to Ali—it was negative. Ali chased her around the yard, cursing and threatening her. "You look like a camel with that hump," he shouted. As soon as he caught up with her she broke loose from him and ran out of the house. Before long she quit working for them. After Khadijeh left Ali was morose for days.

She wondered how her mother felt about her father exactly. Did that futile look that so frequently came to her mother's face point to shattered dreams? She had gotten married when she was only fourteen to a man twice her age. In a wedding photograph she stood next to him, wearing a floor-length dress and a hat, her lips heart-shaped, her hair set in tight curls. She looked more like a daughter than a wife.

Through the oval door Minou could see the sky turning blood-red. Another day lost, bringing her closer to nothing. She floated in time and space. She would end up like her mother. A great sense of loneliness, of claustrophobia, came over her. She had to get out, breathe other air. She decided to go back to school to see who might be there. She would look for Javad Partovi, talk to him finally. There was no reason for her timidity. He had always encouraged her in class, her writing, her comments on other students' compositions. She would go from the courtyard so that her mother would not notice her leaving.

Ali was sitting in the barbershop next door, talking to the owner, a thin, dark man. Minou passed the shop quickly so that Ali would not see her. Tar was spread on one side of Pahlavi Street, in streaks like black tentacles. Traffic moved slowly on the other side. Steam rose from the pavement where shopkeepers had splashed water.

Across from the school the old man who sold pens made from peacock feathers was sitting in front of his shop, looking around. Except for him the street was empty. The school yard was also empty and enveloped in a hazy twilight. The single window of Javad Partovi's office was lit, she immediately noticed. So he was there!

She went into the corridor and paused in front of his office, hesitating. Then she tapped softly on the door.

"Come in, just turn the knob," he said distractedly.

She opened the door and went in. "I came here to..."

He looked up from a book open on his desk and said, "Minou Hakimi, what are you doing at school at this hour?"

"I thought... I might have left my history book."

"Oh!"

"I noticed your lights were on and I thought I'd come in to see you."

"Sit down." He pointed to a chair.

She sat down awkwardly. The whole room was cluttered with books and magazines. Some empty Coca-Cola bottles lay on the floor.

He was looking at her expectantly, waiting for her to tell him what had really brought her to his office.

What could she say to him? She suddenly had nothing to say.

"Have you been working hard?" he asked.

"Yes, with the finals so close."

"Are you going away to college?"

"My parents are against sending me away."

"We could use a college in Ahvāz."

"My brother is studying in the United States, but it's different for me." She was engulfed in the somber mood that had brought her there. "Sometimes I can't bear the thought of another day in Ahvāz—it's bleak, oppressive. Everything is dingy and gray. There's so little to do." She stopped, ashamed. Why should she unburden herself to him, someone she had known for only a few weeks and always in the confinement of the classroom?

"That story you wrote about a girl being sold in a bazaar has come back to me several times. But men have their problems, too. I'd do many things differently if I had the choice."

"Like what?"

"I'd rather not go back to my previous appointment in Abadan. I was in a rut there and wanted to get away, so I took on this job, but your other teacher is returning. There are no openings, not here and not anywhere else decent." His face was slightly flushed. Curls of hair hung over his forehead. He looked extremely attractive. He leaned forward a little. She wished he would reach out and touch her, but his hands remained on his lap. There was an invisible charge between them that felt like a touch. "In Abadan my spirit deadened so slowly that I wasn't even aware of it. But finally I managed to leave."

"The composition class has taken on life since you came. I wish it could go on and on." The words flew out of her.

There was a knock on the door. They both turned around. It was the janitor.

"I have to lock up," he said, looking at Minou suspiciously.

"We'll be out of here in a moment," Javad said.

The janitor walked away.

She and Javad got up. He put some notes on his desk in order and picked up the book he had been reading. "I'll walk out with you," he said.

They walked quietly through the courtyard, which was full of the sound of crickets. Outside, by the door, they paused.

"How are you getting home?" he asked.

"I'm walking back, that way."

"I live in the opposite direction. I've been living with my mother."

"Did you grow up in Ahvāz?" It seemed impossible that she had never seen him before he came to teach there.

"I lived here through high school." In a tone that she thought sounded a little self-conscious he added, "You were just a child when I left Ahvāz to go to the university."

If she could have, she would have stood there for the rest of the evening and listened to the story of his life.

"Are you sure you're going to be all right walking home alone?" he asked.

"I'll go by Pahlavi Street. It's well lit and crowded."

"I guess it isn't that late."

"Good-bye."

"Good-bye."

She turned around once in the middle of the street. He turned around then, too. He waved at her. She waved back.

She walked home rapidly, elated. It was as though she

had resolved something within herself. As she was reaching the house she was suddenly panicked that her parents might have noticed her absence. When she got in, she saw Ali sitting on the porch playing his flute.

"Your mother and father are in their room. They haven't come to dinner yet."

She went directly to her room and shut the door.

6

Then it was the week of the final examinations. Minou worked late into the night, getting no more than a few hours of sleep. In the morning she rushed to school, fearing that she might get there late. The courtyard was filled with talk of having studied the wrong thing, of how hard the examinations they had already taken had been. A bucket of ice water and glasses were set on a table under a tree, and students kept going over, drinking glass after glass.

The night of the last finals there was a school play. Minou sat with Farzin in the auditorium. The play resembled old American musicals. Two dozen girls, wearing striped outfits and tall hats, posed on different parts of the stage and sang. Light played tricks on their faces. The audience hailed the actresses and frequently broke into applause. Some sang with the performers, releasing the tension they had kept in during the examination week.

Javad Partovi was sitting with the other teachers close to the front. Minou kept glancing at him. Since she had gone to see him in his office she had not talked to him alone. She thought she might be able to talk to him after the play, but he left immediately with the other teachers. It occurred to her that she might never see him again.

On the day that the grades were supposed to be posted she and Farzin went to school early and looked for their marks. She had gotten an A in composition and in most other subjects. The good marks only made her despondent. What was the point if she was not going to be able to do anything with them?

"What are we going to do with ourselves now?" she said to Farzin.

"I wish I knew."

She had never been more at loose ends, more aware of uncertainty ahead of her.

During the long days that followed, Minou thought of Javad Partovi frequently. His image mingled with the faces of the men in town smiling and winking at her, the actors she watched on the movie screen. It was evoked by the urgent sound of Western music from the cinema across the street, by the breezy night air. She tried to imagine him in his daily activities now that school was over, but she knew so little about him. She looked for him in public places. At night, walking with her mother on the crowded bridge over the Kārūn River, she imagined him leaning over the railing and staring at the dark water below.

How dismal this summer was. The streets were torpid, flies rampant, buzzing, sucking at people's arms, eyes. The river receded to a thin, slow stream. Homeless men took shelter in doorways or in the shade cast by high walls. Still some of them died of heatstroke.

"It's hot," everyone said. "It's hot, it's hot," they said, as if this were a phenomenon they were encountering for the first time. They drank *dugh* all day long and ate watermelon to quench their thirst. On particularly breezeless days the air smelled heavily of petroleum. People said over and over, "It smells of petroleum."

During the day Minou stayed in her room with the shades and curtains drawn and the fan turned on high. If she went as far as the kitchen to get something, she became soaked with sweat.

Late in the afternoon, when the heat abated somewhat, she and Farzin went for walks. The brightest spots in town for them were the river and the train station. She stood with Farzin on the riverbank or on the platform of the station and dreamed of going away, flowing, floating.

They stopped at the photographer's store on Pahlavi Street and examined the blown-up pictures in its window. Some of them were familiar, faces of people they had seen in town. They had their own photographs taken. It was important to preserve moments of their lives. By doing so they might divert their restlessness into the intense faces of the photographs.

They went into a shop that sold pictures of actors. Farzin bought a few—Barbra Streisand, Paul Newman, Marcello Mastroianni—to add to a large collection of actors' photographs she had pasted in an album.

They strolled in the park or rented rowboats and went across the river. They saw every movie they could. Iranian movies often had the same theme: about a young woman who comes to a large city, from her village, in the hope of a more glamorous life, loses her virginity to a man who later abandons her, and then is forced into becoming a prostitute. Love always ended in disgrace for a woman, sometimes for a man as well. A man could fall in love with the wrong woman also and later become disillusioned with her. Then he would come home, having lost the respect of his family and perhaps an important position in his father's business.

They much preferred the foreign movies and discussed them feverishly. "Elizabeth Taylor was great. I started crying in the middle and couldn't stop," Minou would say. Farzin agreed. They saw parts of themselves caught in the bright flashes of the images on the screen. How could they lead these limited, inhibited lives while that other world existed? They kept saying to each other, "I wish I could go away from here, any place would be better than this."

Outside of the two cinemas men stood watching the girls going by. "You're so pretty," they said to Minou and Farzin. "You have such beautiful hair."

Farzin and Minou looked away, ignoring them. They laughed a lot, another way to give themselves a high, a relief from futility. They laughed at the silly remark a boy made, at a bad story printed in *Setareh*, at the self-satisfied expression on the face of a mutual friend. They laughed at the bumpiness of the bus they took from Farzin's house to Pahlavi Street, making them bend forward and backward.

Minou was not permitted to visit Farzin overnight. Her mother said, "Her brother is your age, people will talk." Farzin's brother was a polite, gentlemanly boy who occasionally accompanied Farzin for a walk on the bridge at night. Minou would go over to Farzin's house in the morning and Ali would pick her up in the evening.

To counteract the boredom, Minou answered an advertisement in the newspaper: "Young girl wanted to dub Italian movie into Persian. Khorshid Studio, 55 Pahlavi Street." She decided to go over and inquire about it.

The studio was on the second floor of a building. She went in and waited in the reception room. Three well-dressed women, who could be singers or actresses, were also waiting. A conversation was going on behind a shut door—several men were talking about their experiences abroad.

"Americans never tell you the truth to your face. They smile at you and then knife you in the back."

"Yes, they have a superficial, impersonal friendliness."

"I like the Italians better. They're more straightforward, like us."

"The French are very arrogant."

"You're right."

The sound track of a movie drowned their voices for a moment. Then the door opened and a man put his head out. The other women did not respond. They seemed to be waiting for someone else. Minou got up and introduced herself to the man and told him she had seen the advertisement. He said his name was Ahmad Khalili. He asked her to go inside with him. In the dim room she could see two other men dressed up in suits like Mr. Khalili. They left when she came in. Mr. Khalili asked her to sit on a chair and say a few words into the microphone as a test. He said he liked her voice. He needed her for a few hours to dub the voice of Sophia Loren in an Italian movie, *Two Women*. Would she be able to do it right then? She said she could.

He projected the movie on the screen and told her to watch the mouth of the actress and to say the words typed on a sheet of paper in time with Sophia Loren's mouth. Minou followed the instructions. She had to repeat it; the second time he was satisfied. He paid her for the job immediately—500 *tomans*—and told her that he would call her if in the future he needed work on other movies.

She walked home, excited at having done something on her own and gotten paid, but as she was reaching her house she realized that she would not be able to tell her

parents about it. They would think of the studio as a cor-
rupting influence and would forbid her to go there
again—she had to hide the money from them.

Two days later her father found out. He came into her
room, looking angry. Mr. Khalili had called and left a
message with him that Minou should go to the studio, that
he was interested in using her to dub another movie.

"Only whores do that kind of thing," her father said.

"I don't see the harm."

"If you don't think there's anything wrong with it, why
did you hide it?"

"I knew you'd object."

"Don't you dare to go to that filthy studio again. I
shouldn't let you see any more movies, I should go through
all your books to make sure you aren't reading the wrong
kind."

"I don't have to listen to you. . . ."

He walked away as though afraid of what might follow.

When Minou was a child she had woken up one morning with an eye infection. Her father sat beside her and examined her eyes. He held her in his arms gently as if afraid
to crush her and took her into the kitchen. He made tea
and a soft-boiled egg for her—her mother and Ali were
out—and he waited with her until she finished eating.
Then he carried her back into bed. "It's chilly here, you'll
catch a cold," he said, covering her with a sheet and kissing
her. He had been the most affectionate with her when she
was weak. She could go to him now and apologize and ask
for forgiveness. But did she want to resort to that? She
stayed in her room, thinking, This is prison, anything is
better than this.

Minou and her parents went to an abandoned orchard
just outside of Ahvāz that had become a popular picnicking
place. It was cool there, shaded with ancient cypresses and

oak trees. Streams flowed through it. They spread a blanket under a tree and Minou, her mother, and her father sat on it while Ali sprayed the slow flies buzzing in the air with a hand pump, leaving a lingering smell of kerosine. Then he went to the stream to fill a pitcher with water. Sparrows chirped at the edge of the stream, dipping their heads in the water. Other families sat in different areas of the garden. Children were playing hopscotch and swinging on ropes they had tied to trees.

"I wish I had asked Narghes and Mehri to come with us. Their husbands would be off work today, too," her mother said.

"I wanted to have a quiet day by ourselves," her father said. "I didn't expect so many people here. I should have known that everyone would swarm here on a day like this."

"There aren't that many places to have a picnic, unless we go much farther out."

"Next time that's what we will do, drive as far away as possible. That reminds me, Ali'd better go and check the car. There are a lot of idle people around today." He called loudly to Ali.

Ali waited for a moment and then got up and walked toward the car. Her father had just bought a Mercedes-Benz for what seemed to be a lot of money, judging by the good care he took of it, keeping it washed all the time, so that its black body was always shiny, not dusty and scratched like the Paykan they used to have.

"Why are you so quiet?" her father asked.

She shrugged. Since the incident of the studio a definite coolness had arisen between her and her father.

"You miss your friend Farzin to chatter with," he said. "What do you talk to her about all the time? I know what, you don't have to tell me. You complain and criticize everything you can think of."

"It's so awful here, in Ahvāz."

"Not that again. It's my fault. I shouldn't have brought it up."

"Relax, it's your day off," her mother told him.

A look of boredom came over her father's face. Her mother looked a little out of her element also. She sniffed the air. "It smells sweet." She added wistfully, "If Sohrab were here he would be full of stories that would make us laugh."

Ali came back. "The car is fine."

Ali helped Minou and her mother spread a tablecloth on top of the blanket and put out the lunch on it. Her father got up and walked away. He came back shortly and they began to eat, Ali by the stream, a little separate from them.

"The fish is good for a change. Did Ali cook it or did you?" her father asked her mother.

"I seasoned it myself. Ali tends to salt it too much."

"It has just the right amount of spices. You used to do all the cooking yourself, remember?"

"How can I forget?"

He smiled. "You were just a little girl when I married you, fourteen years old. Did you know that, Minou?"

"Yes." Minou was uneasy, afraid of a little lecture following, that it was time for her to get married, if the right suitor came along.

A beggar with a goiter on his neck came over and stretched out his hand for food. Minou's mother gave him a piece of chicken on bread. He walked away.

"You shouldn't give them anything or else they'll keep coming," Minou's father said.

"You're right," her mother said.

A woman and three men carrying a sitar, a drum, and a violin took a spot not far from them. They began to play their instruments and one of the men began to sing.

*"Friend, do not listen to those who
 tell you that
I have someone else other than you,
 that
I ever think of anyone else or
 anything else than you...."*

He looked into the woman's eyes and she returned his gaze while he played his sitar faster and louder.

*"I'm not the only one who has fallen
 into the trap of your hair,
For there is a prisoner in each curl
 of your locks."*

A gold tooth in front of his mouth gleamed as he sang, and he looked with an exaggerated expression of desire at the woman's black hair.

A fanatic expression came into Minou's father's face.

"Don't look at them," he said to her.

Minou turned around, not wanting to start an argument in public. Anyway, her mother was right. It would be nearly impossible to change her father's view of things. There was something formidable about him. She envied Farzin for the kind of father she had. She would tickle his feet when he was taking a nap and he would wake, laughing. Even now, at her age, she climbed onto his lap.

The singer's voice became softer and more melancholy.

*"I'm nothing when my body is not
 the abode of your love,
I take your bitterness, love, in
 exchange for emptiness."*

43

The singer would kiss the woman when they were alone,
Minou thought. They would lie together, touch drunkenly,
laugh.

Minou's father had finished eating. He leaned against
the tree and began to smoke a pipe. The musicians stopped
playing. Minou got up. "I'm going for a walk."

"Don't go too far, we'll be leaving soon," her father said.

A cool breeze was blowing and the edge of her dress
swirled around her and clung to her. She opened her
mouth, catching the breeze, closed her eyes to feel its soft
touch against her lids. Her parents seemed far away as if it
were days, instead of minutes, since she was with them.

She came to a crowded spot, where people had gathered
by a little shack that carried goat milk, *dugh*, and bread.
Then she felt a swift, vibrant thrill. Javad Partovi stood
there by the shack, about to buy something. Two old
women, holding their *chadors* tightly, were with him. The
vendor handed them three glasses of bubbling *dugh*. The
two women went to sit by a tree. Javad walked away. He
leaned against a jagged wall, the remnant of a building.
He stood there, unaware of her, with that remote air that
came over him sometimes, as if in order to bear his surroundings he had to withdraw from them for a period of
time.

Finally she went over to him. "Mr. Partovi."

He turned to her, his face instantly lighting up.

"I thought you had left Ahvāz," she said awkwardly.

"I will be leaving soon, at the end of the summer. Are
you here with your family?"

"Yes, they're sitting on the other side."

But he seemed preoccupied by something else. He kept
glancing at the two women. "I'm glad to see you here. I
wanted to contact you, but I wasn't sure how," he said in a
rapid, nervous way. "I thought of writing you a letter or
calling you, but I didn't think it was a good idea."

"You want to talk to me about something?" she asked incredulously.

Two boys ran past them, tugging the strings of kites and giggling. There were many kites floating in the air, several caught in trees. He waited until the sounds of the boys' laughter subsided. Then he said, in a low tone, "Something has been on my mind for a while. I'd like to send my mother over to speak to your parents, if that's all right with you...."

It seemed like a long time before she said, "This is such a surprise."

"There are no problems, I hope."

"No, no, this is just unexpected."

"I was afraid your parents might have promised you to someone." His face at that moment was free of all burdens and reflected, transparently, happiness.

But Minou could not quite let go of herself. Something incredible lay at the core of it all, it was so utterly odd. How long had he been thinking about it, when did the idea come to him? If they had been alone she would have asked him all these questions.

"I'd better go now. They're waiting for me." He pointed to the two women. "I'll send them to your house soon."

He walked away.

If forced to imagine a marriage to this man, she would have seen many long tutoring sessions in which his admiration for her would gradually grow. There would be shy glances. Their hands would ultimately brush as she passed him a pencil. He would finally declare his love, but immediately afterward would say that they would never see each other again because he was too old (although he was younger than most of her suitors). She would agree sadly, but his passion would overcome him and he would kiss her. Then, mortified, he would leave, but eventually he would return and beg her to marry him despite his age.

She went over and over the brief, unexpected encounter. Finally she constructed a scenario that explained his sudden proposal. She imagined that his story was parallel to her own. His parents were pressing him to get married. Attractive as he was, he was shy and there were no women in his life. He had devoted himself to literature, but he had reached a point where he was ready for marriage. Like her, he refused to allow his parents to select a wife for him, but his only contact with women was at school. The female teachers were all married and there were no students mature enough and sophisticated enough to be his wife, not until that night in his office when he discovered how much they had in common. Maybe her composition about a woman being sold as a slave or something she said had made him look at her in a new light. In any case he had asked her to marry him.

At first, as she had expected, her father objected to the wedding: they would not be able to ask for enough *mehrieh* with his income as a teacher; he was of a good enough family (Javad's father, who had died years ago in a car accident, had been employed in a high post at the Ministry of Education), but would he be able to support her and their children comfortably?

"How will you manage if you have a son who wants to go to college in Europe or the United States?" He looked perplexed. "What if one of them has a major illness? You won't have enough money to take him to Tehran or abroad."

"You're trying to think of everything."

"I'm looking out for your interests. We have to be practical—you can't live on air."

"Javad isn't poor."

"I can't stand children who disobey their parents."

"I'm not disobeying you."

"What are you doing, then?"

"I'm doing something for myself."

"If he divorces you for any reason, the seventy thousand *tomans mehrieh,* which is all we can ask, won't go very far."

Then he seemed lost in another thought. Perhaps he recalled his own disobediences. He had gone into law instead of his father's business, had married much later in life than his family had hoped.

As she looked at him, it struck her how good-looking he must have been as a young man. His rather pudgy face hid regular, fine features—dark, penetrating eyes, a thatch of thick hair, now gray. He must have been as vain then as he was proud now.

Her mother and father had rarely conveyed the impression of matrimonial happiness, but there was a definite dependency between them as if one would wither away without the other. Their mutual dependence had often made her feel excluded and lonely. Now there was the added fear that the two of them together would wipe out her will. She pleaded with her mother to argue on her side. Her mother could not make any promises.

"You must tell Father that I won't marry anyone else. Javad is the only man I will marry."

"I'll tell him," was all her mother said.

But there were several days of talks behind doors between her mother and father, and finally her father consented. He said to Minou, in a sardonic tone, "I can't keep a girl around too long, but I hope that at least you understand you're settling for less than you deserve. Other, better-established men with much more money have asked for you."

48

Throughout the engagement Minou saw Javad only once, when he came to their house to visit with her father. The two men sat in the living room and played backgammon and talked.

She could see from Javad's stiff posture as she glanced at him from the hallway that he was tense. After a while, as he and her father drank arak, he relaxed a bit. He laughed with her father as though they were old friends. She tried to catch their conversation.

"The poetry published these days is rubbish, total self-indulgence," her father said.

"Much of it isn't good, but still we do need to let in fresh voices."

"We're constantly imitating the West even though we have had the greatest poets in the world—Hafiz, Saadi."

Javad was silent. No doubt he found her father dogmatic. Her father spoke with finality in his voice, leaving little room for anyone to contradict him.

He went on, "We've been imitating the West in so many ways. Some of it hasn't been so bad—I'm glad women aren't required by the law to wear the *chador* as they used to—but I'm against the licentiousness propagated in Western books and movies."

"Your son is in the United States; what's he studying?" Javad asked.

"He keeps changing his mind. He thought about medicine for a while, then law, now he doesn't know at all."

"I assume he likes it there."

"He has his criticisms. He says they have good facilities, particularly for science, but he thinks the people are cold."

"Then he will come back after he's finished?"

"I'm counting on it."

The rest of the conversation was carried on in low tones. What kind of revelations did they make to one another?

Minou had the same feeling as when her father talked in whispers with clients, that there was a world totally hidden from her. She hated to see Javad as a part of that alien world.

They left the practical matter of the wedding to the women, to Minou's mother and Javad's mother and aunt. The three women worked as a harmonious team. Minou went into the room to serve them tea. She sat with them briefly. Javad's relatives, both wearing *chadors*, reminded her of her aunts. She was instantly comfortable in their presence, even under their scrutinizing eyes, but she was quiet with them—she knew them even less than she knew Javad.

She looked at herself in the mirror, examining her wedding dress—white satin covered with pearls—her makeup, the curls that Aunt Mehri had set in her hair earlier in the day. She and her mother had argued over the dress. Her mother wanted it to be more elaborate, with sequins on it and a layer of gauze to give it extra body. This dress was a compromise, still a little fancier than Minou wanted, but it had white-on-white embroidered flowers at the neckline that she liked. How quickly it had all happened! She kept looking at the golden hands of her watch. In a few moments she would be married to Javad. Her room was filled with frilly objects—sheets, pillowcases, quilted bedspreads—a part of her dowry that her mother had begun to put together frantically when the details of the wedding were settled.

As soon as the wedding arrangements began, Minou had moments of ecstasy. Her days were full of unexpected turns, her future rang with promise. Yet waiting, at this stage, was excruciating. It was four o'clock, the time that the ceremony was supposed to take place, but Javad had not arrived. What could be holding him up? The orchard where he proposed came to her mind with an aura of unreality—Javad standing next to the jagged wall talking to her nervously.

Through the door she could see last-minute preparations being made. In a shady corner of the hall Ali was crushing a block of ice with a hammer, picking up the pieces from the ground and putting them in a plastic container. The fish he had cleaned lay on top of one another in a basket, their discarded scales spangling on the ground. Zahra, a woman who came in several times a week to help Minou's mother with the housework, was assisting the waiter they had hired for the occasion. They put dishes and silverware on the tables in the living room and the hall. Her mother and father put flowers and glasses for drinks on the tables. Javad had insisted on a small wedding. They expected about sixty people, mostly relatives.

Minou's aunts came in. They were both dressed up. Narghes was wearing a pale green georgette dress with a dark velveteen pattern embossed on it. She kept it with her other good dresses in a red felt-covered trunk in the basement of her house. Mehri had on a silk dress of various shades of blue.

Aunt Mehri sat down on a chair. Aunt Narghes moved around Minou, looking at her wedding dress. "The inner layer is a little longer than the outer one. He hasn't done a good job even though he's supposed to be the best tailor in town."

"I thought he was being careful," Minou said.

"It doesn't matter, you can't see it," Mehri said.

"It will only take me a minute to hem it. Let me do it for you," Narghes said, sitting down at Minou's feet. "You don't have to take off the dress." She took out a needle from the sewing box lying in a corner and threaded it. Then she began to hem the dress, making Minou turn slowly.

"That's much better," Narghes said, getting up and ex-

amining the hem. She took out an embroidered handkerchief from her purse and gave it to Minou. "You may need
it to wipe away your tears."

Minou's mother came in, dressed up in a long royal-blue
dress, high heels, and a gold necklace and bracelet. Her
hair was set in a permanent, in tight little curls; her lips
were red with lipstick.

"Javad is late," she said. "The *aghound* is already here."

Minou looked at her watch again. It was ten minutes
after four.

"How selfish men can be," her mother said.

"Men are men. They do what they want," Narghes said.

How often Minou had heard these remarks from her
mother and aunts. She tried to shut them out, but still she
was sucked into the somber mood that quickly filled the air
like poisonous mist.

Was Javad having second thoughts about the wedding?
She wished, for an instant, that she had never met him.
But at some level of her existence she already possessed
him, permanently.

"You ought to have listened to your father," her mother
said.

"Anything could have happened to delay him for a few
moments," she said, trying to push down her own anxiety.

"Remember Homayoon *khan* was late on your wedding
night?" Mehri said.

"Those were different times. His horsecart had broken
down," her mother said, sitting on the bed and looking
apprehensive.

Minou sat next to her, leaning a little toward her for
comfort. Her mother patted her head. "We're upsetting
you."

"You are so short that on your wedding night our mother
had to lift you off the ground and put you into the carriage," Mehri went on.

"I kept crying all night. I was a little afraid of Homayoon. He looked so stern. Our mother kept saying, 'You'll get used to him in no time.'"

Minou's father coughed outside, and Narghes and Mehri reached for their *chadors* and put them on. He came in. He was dressed up in a blue linen suit.

"What happened to the bridegroom?" he said. "I knew the marriage was a mistake."

Minou avoided his eyes.

"The shame we will have to face, if this falls through," her mother said.

Her father walked away, shaking his head.

"It's so difficult to tell young people what's good or bad," her mother said to her aunts.

"The God that gave them to you will protect them," Narghes said.

"What do they know about God?" her mother said. "They try to take their lives into their own hands."

"Stop talking about me. I'm in the room with you," Minou said, trying to keep her voice from sounding exasperated.

A sudden silence followed. Minou strummed her fingers on the arm of the chair, anxious, impatient.

Ali came to the door. "The bridegroom is here. He's in the living room with the *aghound*." He also was dressed up, in a white shirt and black pants.

"Thank God," her mother said.

They all got up and followed Ali to the living room. Javad, the *aghound*, Javad's mother and aunt, and Minou's father were all sitting on chairs, waiting. The edge of the *aghound*'s long robe lay creased on the floor. Javad was wearing a white suit and a blue tie. Everyone greeted one another.

"I'm sorry," Javad said to Minou. "It took me longer to get ready than I thought."

"I was wondering what had happened." She sat beside him. Her mother, Ali, and her aunts sat next to his mother and aunt. At last the pleasure of the occasion began to glow in her.

Javad's mother whispered something to her mother, perhaps explaining the delay.

The *aghound* asked, "Shall I begin?"

"Go ahead," Minou's father said.

The *aghound* began to say the sermon. It lasted for a few moments and then he recited a surah from the Koran. He had hennaed his beard and fingernails. His black eyes flashed. He pronounced each word distinctly, gutturally. After he was finished he turned to Javad and Minou and said, "Now you're wedded and have duties to one another—of faithfulness, of procreation. You, Mr. Partovi, will have to provide for her. Marriage is a sacred act. You enter a holy realm. May this last forever, may God give you many children, He whose will watches over everything. May His blessing be eternally with you."

There was a flurry of talk, everyone congratulating and blessing the bride and groom. Mehri and Narghes came over to Minou. They held a cloth above her head and grated sugar into it to sweeten the marriage. Javad put two rings on Minou's fingers, a plain gold one and an old-fashioned one with a ruby stone that he said had been in his family for a long time.

Minou's father asked the *aghound,* "Would you care to stay and celebrate with us?"

"It's kind of you to ask, but I have other duties today."

"At least have some tea."

"Thank you, but I must leave." He got up.

Her father handed him an envelope, which he took and put in the pocket of his long robe. He turned to Javad and Minou. "God bless you."

They all said good-bye to him and he left.

Guests began to come in, one by one, all dressed up, some with their clothes only barely revealed under their *chadors.* Children were dressed up, too, in immaculate, perfectly ironed clothes, the girls wearing ribbons in their hair and white stockings. The men wore suits and starched white shirts. Quickly the air was filled with a babble of conversation and laughter. Women whispered comments about the bride and the groom and about the way the party was handled. Drinks spilled, a glass shattered, a child began to cry and his mother rocked him on her shoulder. The guests walked around freely from table to table, from the room to the corridor, into the courtyard. Some of the young boys went to the balcony and looked at the activity on the street.

Narghes' and Mehri's husbands sat together, smoking the water pipes they had specially requested and looking on rather quietly, tired from their day of work at their jobs—Narghes' husband was the owner of a gift shop and Mehri's part owner of a thread factory. They were better friends with one another than with Minou's father, being more old-fashioned and devout than he.

Mehri's three daughters sat near Minou, watching her with curiosity. They were all pretty in a robust way, a little plump, with ruddy faces. Still in high school, they already had thoughts about marriage. They dreamed of crystal, silk, gold, and silver, of children surrounding them, of a life of comfort in one another, of interdependency.

Her mother and father joined the guests, talking with them and asking them if they needed their drinks replenished. The anxiety had lifted from her parents' faces.

A belly dancer, hired along with a small band of musicians, arrived. The guests began to come inside. The musicians played the violin, a drum, and cymbals. The dancer began to dance with wide, sinuous steps. Music flowed out gaily, in a rush. People had gathered on rooftops across the

street, dark shapes looking on. A photographer went
around and took pictures. The dancer went into a frenzy of
movements, her whole body shaking. Sequins gave out
sharp flashes on her already shimmering satin dress. Her
black hair and eyes were pools of darkness against the glitter. She wore opaque silver stockings, which showed
through the slit of her skirt. Finally she threw herself on
the floor, lay there for an instant, and then got up to loud
applause. She bent backward, her head touching her feet,
her body curved like a bridge. She rose and resumed dancing to a louder and faster rhythm. The guests clapped and
snapped their fingers. Men threw coins at her. Javad
watched with a weary, remote expression. Minou felt
remote, too, thinking of a life shared with Javad, of the
emotions that drew her to him forcefully. Supplementing
her love for him was a sense of gratitude. She shuddered to
think what her life would have been like if not for
him—drifting around her parents' house until she was
forced into marrying someone.

She turned to look at Javad.

He said, "I can't wait until this is over."

"I know what you mean."

"You look at me sometimes as if I were someone else."

"I don't understand."

"You idealize me." He smiled. "I'm like any other human
being, with faults."

She was at a loss for what to say. A kind of hurt came
over her.

Seeing that hurt on her face, he held her hand in his for
a moment. "What can I expect? We've hardly had the opportunity to be alone together."

The dancer bowed a few times and left the room, accompanied by one of the musicians. The whole dance had
lasted no longer than an hour, but it had made a deep dent

in the random noise and activity of the evening. After that there was a steady quieting down.

Ali, Zahra, and the waiter cleared the tables and put out more food. Minou's father refilled the drinks. The two remaining musicians began to play a soft waltz. Javad and Minou were prodded to dance by Javad's cousin, who had been talking and laughing all evening. They danced to the applause of the guests—they held each other at a distance for propriety. In a corner some young girls and boys were dancing, girls with girls, boys with boys, the opposite sexes forbidden to touch.

In a few moments Minou and Javad went back to their seats. The guests began to leave one by one. Minou's friends Farzin, Mahroo, and Mahvash, among the few friends who had been invited, came over to her and Javad. They were quiet, shy with Javad. Then they left, too. Minou walked them to the stairway, leading to the outside door.

"We won't be able to talk every day anymore," Farzin said, despair creeping into her tone. "I have no idea what I will be doing with myself now that you're leaving."

Minou could not help thinking how miraculously she had been saved from despair by Javad. She kissed her friends one by one. Then they went down the stairs, whispering among themselves. She did not envy their confidences. She had Javad to confide in. When she had first told Farzin about the marriage, Farzin said, "Now you're going to find out all about him."

As she returned to the room, the musicians were leaving. Soon it was time for her and Javad to depart to his mother's house.

Relatives stood in a cluster on the sidewalk as Minou and Javad and his mother and aunt got into a car belonging to Javad's cousin. Javad, Minou, and Javad's mother sat in the back, Javad's cousin and aunt in the front. Hundreds of moths fluttered around the streetlamps.

Minou's mother was weeping. "She was my only child at home and she's going away," she said. "I'm not strong enough for it."

"We'll take good care of her," Javad's mother remarked.

"What an ugly bride," Minou's father said jokingly. He leaned over and kissed her. Then her mother kissed her.

Javad's cousin drove off. A line of five other cars, filled with relatives, followed. Green leaves and flowers were strung on the cars. Someone began to play the tambourine in one of the cars, and a few people sang a wedding song. Passersby stopped on the sidewalks to take a look at the bride and the groom.

"You must have been worried when we were late," Javad's mother said to Minou.

"I wondered what could have happened."

"The truth is, Javad was nervous. He kept changing shirts and looking at himself in the mirror like a young boy."

They all laughed.

Minou was filled with that anxious, beating joy that had come over her often since Javad had proposed.

"All the rituals!" Javad said.

"You like to go your own way," his mother remarked, not critically but in amused praise. She turned to Minou again. "I'm happy he finally met someone he's willing to settle down with. I can see why. You're just fine. Young and pretty."

"Even men who go abroad to study usually come back to marry our own girls," Javad's aunt said. "We have cousins in Germany. They both came back, married two young women, and took them back. They said German girls don't make good wives."

"I wish my husband were alive to see Javad getting married," Javad's mother said. "It was difficult to raise a son without a father to look after him. I did my best to be both mother and father to him, to give him whatever he asked for."

"May his soul rest in heaven," Javad's cousin said.

"At least it was quick," Javad's aunt said. "Remember all the days my husband lay ill, in agony with kidney problems? Operation after operation did him no good."

"It prepared you for the end," Javad's mother said.

"Let's not talk about these sorrowful things," Javad's

cousin remarked. "It's absurd to even think about them at this festive occasion."

"Sorrow is a part of life," Javad's mother said. But she went on to another subject. "I wish you two weren't going away so soon. I'd have liked to get acquainted with Minou."

Minou and Javad were planning to leave in two days for a short vacation and then go on to Abadan. His teaching would start in ten days.

"You'll get a chance later, on visits," Javad said, patting his mother's arm. He seemed fond of his mother and aunt in an easy, effortless way, taking their love for granted.

They reached the street where Javad's mother and aunt lived together. Javad's cousin stopped the car by the house to let everyone out and said good-bye to them. More of Javad's relatives, about fifteen men and women, got out of the other cars. Then all the cars left.

Javad's mother opened the door and they went in, passing through a hallway and entering a courtyard. The sky was luminous with stars. Javad's aunt and the other relatives said good night and went into the rooms on the other side of the courtyard, where they would sleep on mattresses spread on the floor, the men separate from the women. Then Javad's mother led him and Minou to their bedroom. She paused outside the room and kissed them good night.

"Now you're on your own," she said with a smile.

Inside, Javad took off his jacket and sighed with relief. "I'm glad that's all over," he said.

"I know what you mean," Minou answered. But she was shy now that she was alone with him.

The bed was neatly made with a dark blue and white bedspread. A pair of silk pajamas and a satin robe lay near the head of the bed and two pairs of slippers were placed at the foot. Vases of flowers were set everywhere—on the mantelpiece, on a wooden chest, on the floor. A large, heavy mirror with a gold frame hung on one wall. Minou stared at her reflection next to Javad's in the mirror. She waited for a kiss—the miracle of the kiss—that would transform her into womanhood. Her mind for the moment would not go further than a kiss.

He smiled at her. "You were a student in my class and now you're here with me as my wife."

"I was thinking about that all evening."

"I liked you from the beginning," he said. "An intense, curious girl."

"I kept staring at you in class, wondering..."

He put his arm around her waist lightly. Then he pulled her to his chest. She was aware of the texture of his shirt, his flesh underneath it. He kissed her lips, her throat. She had the feeling of being lost in a pool of sensations, flowing and feathery. He let go of her and said, "Let me turn off the light."

Soon she would be lying next to him in bed. How extraordinary that experience would be. What would she feel precisely, more of the same sensations that his kisses had evoked?

"This is better," he said in the darkness.

In the dim room she could still see the outline of his body as he undressed. She began to take off her clothes, too. She groped for her robe on the bed and put it on.

He pulled off the bedspread, then reached for her hand and led her into the bed. For a moment he just held her quietly. He was completely naked. A lonely feeling came over her as he began to take off her robe. "It's like dying," Narghes had said. Mehri had said, "It's going to hurt." Narghes had advised her not to give in to him the first night, not to appear eager.

"Relax, I won't do anything you don't want me to."

The mere sound of his voice comforted her. She moved closer to him, letting go of herself. She wanted to give herself to him totally, whatever he wanted.

He caressed her, her breasts, her thighs.

"Am I hurting you?"

"No."

She pulled away a little and looked at his face, shadowy in the dark. Then her eyes moved to the curtains. For an instant she had the feeling that someone was looking in, watching. Her mother had once said to her that mothers always looked in on their son's wedding to see how the bride behaved. She had heard of women faking virginity, having their hymen sewn or a capsule full of pigeon blood inserted in their vagina by doctors specializing in this, and of women divorced by their husbands because they had been found out not to be virgins. Some families insisted on keeping a handkerchief with the bride to dip into the blood as proof, something that would be kept by the bride's mother.

She hid her face in Javad's chest, deciding not to care. His hand was moving downward, slowly, making her body vibrate with a kind of incredible, startled pleasure. Her own hand moved along his body, as though of her own volition, obeying his hand. Then with the same incredible ease, his body entwined with hers, locking into it. She was not hurt—but she discovered from the stains on the sheets in the morning that she had bled.

So this was it, what she and Farzin had speculated about, what her aunts had warned her against. She fell into a dream state. She was not sure when exactly she fell asleep.

She woke up and reached for him immediately but he was not there. The apprehension that had struck her at his being late for the wedding swept over her again. She sat up and looked around the room. He was sitting on the armchair, looking out through the gauzy curtain.

"Javad," she called, "can't you sleep?"

"You're up?" He paused, then said, "I can't face going back to Abadan. The thought of it kept me up most of the night."

She said, "What bothers you so much about Abadan?"

"It was just the pattern of my life, the same faces all the time, the same routine."

She was cold, exposed. She pulled up the comforter to her chest. He came back into the bed and they lay close to each other.

"How do you feel?" he asked, caressing her hair.

"Fine."

She waited for him to tell her he loved her. She was on the brink of saying she loved him, but shyness held her back. Was that what also kept him from expressing himself more openly? But the feeling was all there, changing her, transforming her. The change was more like a birth or a death than a marriage. She felt herself lifted, magically. She could guess what Abadan was going to be like: a small, hot city on the border with Iraq, a city filled with oil tanks and derricks, slightly larger, slightly more Western than Ahvāz. Still she could not suppress images of wide, tree-lined boulevards, tall apartment buildings, grassy parks.

He put his hand on her arm, rubbing it gently. She sensed a difference in his touch from the night before, with desire drained from it. She was drained, too. Her body ached now. Light was gathering behind the curtains.

"I'm getting dressed." He got out of the bed.

"I will, too."

She could hear the murmur of voices, footsteps in the courtyard. It was like the magical dawns of childhood when she woke to the voices of her parents and relatives, talking and laughing at breakfast, and was filled with a sense of security that life had gone on while she had been asleep. Soon it would be full daylight and a stream of visitors would begin to come in.

Minou sat in a chair stiffly, in her lavender organdy dress and matching lavender shoes, while the guests leaned against cushions on the rug. Javad was with the men in another room. Children mostly played in the courtyard, some stayed in the room close to their mothers.

Presents, brought over by relatives, lay in one corner to be opened later. Fruits, sweets, and nuts, heaped on platters, were set in different places around the room. Once again there was the jingle of crystal and of silver dishes, the shimmer of silk and satin dresses. The aroma of spices, turmeric, saffron, dill, came in from the kitchen, where lunch was being cooked. Glasses of *sharbat* were filled constantly by Javad's mother and aunt. The two sisters talked to each other incessantly as they worked. They would not let Minou help. She had tried earlier to wash the sheets, stained with blood and semen, but her mother-in-law had taken them away from her. "Don't worry about it. I'll wash them later. You're a guest." Minou let go reluctantly.

The house had a coziness about it that her parents' house lacked, with fewer, more closely set together rooms, stained-glass transoms. The courtyard was shaded by palm and tamarind trees.

Older members of the family came in a little later. Most of them had not been present at the wedding, some because they were too religious to sit through all the music and dance, some because they did not like to go anywhere at night. They sat in a row, leaning against pillows. They were quiet, too low in energy perhaps to talk. One of them had no teeth, and when she did speak her mouth gaped like a hole.

Minou missed her own grandmother. Would she have approved of Javad? Men were creatures she could not quite understand. "I used to feel bad about not having a son, but what would I do with a boy? How would I have raised him after your grandfather died?"

Javad's mother gave Minou a bag of photographs to look at. Javad's grandfathers in tall felt hats and crude suits, his father an older replica of Javad, women relatives mostly in *chadors*, only a part of their faces showing. His mother and aunt as young girls, looking lively and robust, very different from their present thin, rather fretful appearance. She would not have recognized them if they had not been identified by their names written underneath. What happens to women as they grow older? she wondered. There were many pictures of Javad—as a little boy holding a pitcher and watering the plants, on his bicycle, climbing a tree. Then the older Javad, dressed up in a suit and a hat, graduating from college, standing beneath a tall mountain, squinting in the sun. In one photograph he stood with a man and a woman on a stairway. The woman was standing between the two men, her arms around their waists. All of them were laughing in an abandoned way. Minou had a twinge of jealousy of Javad's past, the women he must have known. He was much more experienced than she, had seen more. Last night in bed his movements had been sure and confident.

Some of Minou's relatives came in, her parents, aunts, uncles. The men quickly joined the other men. As the last man left the room, the women sighed with relief. Those who wore *chadors* let them drop over their shoulders. Minou let herself be engulfed by the barrage of jumbled conversation around her that had begun to gather momentum.

"The bride and groom will be on their own, with neither mother going with them."

"They will manage."

"Setting up a house all on their own won't be easy."

"She's so sweet-looking."

"She's lovely."

"Not forward-looking, as some girls are these days."

"He's such a nice man, gentle and considerate."

"Yes."

"He's taken after his late father."

"It's good he waited until he found just the right girl."

An airplane droned in the sky. There were sounds of rapid footsteps and giggling—children playing in the courtyard. The outside door kept opening and banging shut.

"She's the serious type, like Javad."

"Until he met her, he kept saying he wouldn't get married."

"His mother is very happy he decided to get married finally."

Minou's mother came over and whispered to her, "You're fidgeting. Relax, be still."

"I'm tired of sitting like this." She wished the day were over and she could be with Javad.

They planned to spend a few days in Khoram Abad, a small half-Arab, half-Persian village, stopping first in Band Gir, a town with many historic sights. They drove Javad's cousin's car along the river.

Except for the distant purple mountains, the horizon was clear. Berries and plantains and sugar reeds grew wild beside the roads. They passed a high dam, which made a white foaming waterfall of the river, groves of quince trees with their fruit a shade darker than the sun shining on them, a wheat field. Two horses, held by a rope over a man's shoulder, went round and round in a corner of the field, threshing wheat.

In Band Gir, Javad parked the car and they began to walk. Children played on the sidewalks of the narrow, winding streets. Cows and goats grazed on the grassy roofs of bungalows.

They visited the castle on the hill just outside of the town, going in through a massive stone gate and a garden. The garden was filled with overgrown weeds and ancient trees with bent and twisted branches. The castle itself was mostly in ruins, with mutilated pillars and steps, a chipped tower full of pigeons, but the inside walls were intact, covered with a bas-relief of flowers, fruit, suns, and fighting animals. The high, arched ceilings had also remained whole. Their footsteps echoed loudly as they went from room to room. A dry wind blew in through the openings that once had been windows.

Centuries ago a shah had begun to build the castle as a shrine for Mohammed. When he saw how beautiful it was he changed it into a residence for himself. God had brought death upon him for his greed.

They climbed up to the turret and stood by the window looking out for a while. The whole town had a transient look. Only the glistening blue and gold domes in the distance seemed real.

People below looked like fish darting back and forth on the surface of water. The late sun made little dots on Javad's face. A patch of hair trembled on his forehead with the wind. She leaned her head on his shoulder. There was no question, she thought: what she felt for him was the most important thing in the world. It had absolute control over her mood.

They walked back to the car on a different street. On the asphalted ground, beside a pile of broken masonry, something was written in chalk. They paused to read it: "Gently, Brother, gently, pray!" The handwriting was clear and careful.

"It's from a poem by Omar Khayyám," Javad said. "Do you know it?"

Minou shook her head.

He began to recite the poem.

> *"For in the Market-Place, one Dusk*
> > *of Day,*
> *I watched the Potter thumping his*
> > *wet Clay:*
> *And with its all-obliterated Tongue*
> *It murmur'd—'Gently, Brother,*
> > *gently, pray!'"*

His recitation of the poem, the fact that he knew it by heart, touched her. It was as though he were her teacher again. She moved closer to him and put her arm inside his. He stopped and kissed her on the mouth.

In a few moments they left Band Gir. They reached Khoram Abad in the afternoon. They passed a square with a few shops, carrying simple things, rice, sugar, beans, displayed in large quantities, a public bath, a mosque. Then they entered a more residential section with houses, some attached to orchards, lining narrow, interwoven lanes.

They stayed in a room they rented in a house. Overlooking a large orchard, it was airy and sparsely furnished with a rug, a mattress on the floor, and a wooden chair. The walls were smudged with soot from the smoke of kerosine lamps. A Koran lay on a windowsill.

That evening they sat outside with the owner, leaning against cushions set on a rug-covered platform. The owner's wife climbed up, carrying, on a tray, a bowl of peeled, sliced melon and a samovar with a teapot simmering on it. The samovar hissed monotonously. The farmer asked Javad many questions, his wrinkled, sunburned face intense with curiosity. Was it true that in other countries farmers could afford a car, a radio, that they all knew how to read and write?

Javad answered his questions patiently.

The farmer's wife asked Javad if he knew of new cures for diseased cows. "Two of our neighbors' cattle just died. The veterinarian was unable to cure them."

"I'm sorry but I don't know," Javad said.

The woman gave Javad and Minou each a large piece of dried, pressed apricot, which she took out of a tin box and unfolded.

"It's from the tree there," the farmer said. "That tree is in such good health."

Javad and Minou ate the apricot slowly. Minou was filled with intense happiness, as if all her wishes had been fulfilled. The outline of the wooden house against the sky, the flowers and the shrubs, the variety of fruit—grapes, quinces, dates—on the trees delighted her. It was like that dawn of her childhood when she had awoken next to her grandmother in the woods among trees and flowers wet with dew. She had gotten up and walked barefoot on the damp ground, quietly, lest she wake anyone. She had touched the gum of the trees, picked the dewdrops with the tips of her fingers, smelled the shrubs with their strange crimson fruit.

And like that other time her grandmother had taken her to visit some relatives in Tabrīz. Distant cousins, aunts and uncles she had never met before, came over to the large house. They all fussed over Minou, kissing her, giving her presents. An aunt made noodles for soup, another made halvah. Heavy darkened pots steamed on fires all day. She went in and out of the house with her young cousins. They explored the neighborhood together, climbed trees, caught large, flying insects and tied their legs to strings. Then they all sat around a long tablecloth spread on the floor, passing the plates of food, each solicitous, making sure that the others had a taste of everything. She could not recall what that room looked like but could still hear the hum of laughter and talk, the sense of warmth and well-being.

In this idyllic place, sitting next to Javad, she could feel the best of her past and the present as one harmonious experience.

During the three days they spent in Khoram Abad they took walks, rowed boats across the river, watched the vivid sunsets. They bathed in mineral springs partitioned by a wall into separate sections for men and women.

They talked on and on, about how much happier they were since they met, how hard it was to imagine life now without each other, and how odd were the hundreds of little coincidences and decisions that had brought them together.

"You know that night, when you came to my office, you looked so innocent and yet I could sense a strength in you. I thought how nice it would be to live with you," he said.

"For a long time in class I wasn't sure what you thought of me."

"How could that be? I was always focusing on you, addressing you."

"I wasn't sure if I wasn't reading something into it."

"I remember what you wore that night when you came to my office, a dark green dress with leaf designs on it."

"That was what I wore the day of the picnic, when I ran into you in the orchard."

"You're right."

"As soon as you came into the class we knew you were going to be different from all the other teachers," she said.

"You talked about me?"

"All the time."

She was standing in the shade of a tree. He said, "That light makes your eyes look black."

"Would you like it if my eyes were black all the time?" She realized that she still clung to his words as she had done in the classroom.

"No, you just look more intense that way."

There were no good restaurants in the village and they came back to their room to eat the meals that the farmer's wife prepared for them—lemon-mint-flavored chicken, bread, cheese—Minou had seen her making the cheese by filling a sack with half-curdled milk and hanging it on a tree overnight for the water to drain out.

A breeze always blew at night. They could hear the trees crashing into one another, doors banging and banging. The moon sailed rapidly across the sky. Jackals howled. They lay in bed, talking, making love, listening to the sounds outside. Minou could feel the charge between Javad and herself, the desire, and she wished she could stay there, in that sparse room, forever.

She submitted to his embraces as if she were in a trance. She forgot her own boundaries, becoming lost in him. How close happiness and unhappiness were sometimes! The essence of both was an ache. Both, when at their height, made her feel disoriented and shapeless.

At dawn they woke to the crowing of roosters, mingling with the voice of the muezzin calling people to prayers. They lay in bed and watched the light spread into the room.

The ship began to glide slowly as they approached Abadan. Minou sat beside Javad. He was quiet—grave, inward. They looked at the Kārūn River, foamy white around the boat. Fluffy clouds hung low in the sky. Minou was full of anticipation. She would set up a house, explore Abadan with Javad.

Ali had come along to help them get settled. He leaned against the railing, looking out also. It was her mother's idea for him to stay with them until Minou found someone else.

It was almost dusk. Some of the passengers lined up on the platform to pray, the men separate from the women, bending, reclining, and rising with the same timing and rhythm, following a man who stood in front and prayed aloud.

> *Ever forgiving, ever kind*
> *We worship only You; only You we*
> *   seek for*
> *Friendship*
> *Lead us to the true path*
> *The path of those to whom you have*
> *   given your*
> *Blessings. . . .*

The boat pulled into the shore. The wharf teemed with sailors, porters, taxi drivers, relatives waiting. The faces were blurred by a thick fog and the air smelled heavily of petroleum from the refineries. Fishermen's shacks, lit from the inside, looked as if they were floating.

Javad, Minou, and Ali disembarked, each carrying a suitcase. The rest of their luggage would be delivered to them in the morning. Javad hailed a taxi.

They passed through dim lanes and came out into a gloomy, dusty square with little shops and food stalls. Beggars stood in every corner asking for money, their voices nasal and sharp. Women, holding their *chadors* around their faces, leaned out of windows of houses. Children sat in doorways playing with marbles or stones.

Then they entered a section where modern houses stood alongside old ones. A full moon dangled close to the edge of the rooftops. Everything was startlingly bright. Minou could see the dates on palm trees. Two rabbits ran in and out of the grass-covered backyard of a Western-style house.

"That's our street," Javad said, pointing to a narrow lane.

Minou looked out, excited at the prospect of living in this new place with Javad.

At the house, Javad paid the driver and the three of them got out.

Inside, he gave Minou and Ali a tour. The house, subsidized by the school where he taught, was rather luxurious. The kitchen and the two bathrooms had been modernized by the Englishmen who had lived there once. A servant's room stood on the other side of the courtyard. The furniture was modern, mostly of dark wood. A few tapestries and plates hung on walls. The man Javad had hired to take care of the house had left everything in order—the floors swept and washed, the furniture dusted, the refrigerator filled with food. Rubber plants and cacti stood in blue ceramic pots in each room.

This was where Javad had lived by himself before he came to teach in Ahvāz. It was as she had expected. It was modern enough, nice enough. Then why this leaden depression, the heavy weighting of her arms, which she could hardly lift? She thought what she was feeling was homesickness, but if her mother, her father, her whole family were there at that moment she would have felt equally bad or worse. Somehow she sensed, only a bare hint of it, that Javad's heart was not in the house. He, too, was depressed, and perhaps his depression had preceded hers.

Ali went to his room, and Javad and Minou to their bedroom. Javad took off his shirt and put it over the arm of a chair. She could see dark tufts of hair under his arms. His skin was honey-colored.

He turned around and saw her watching him. He came over to her and pulled her to his chest.

There was a knock on the door.

"It must be Hassan."

Another knock sounded, more loudly. Javad went to the door. Minou could hear a heated conversation. Several people were arguing, it seemed, about something Javad had neglected.

Javad came back and said, "I have to go out for an hour or so, I'm sorry about it."

"Where are you going?"

"They want me to read over some articles for this newspaper we do together before it goes to press."

"What newspaper? You never told me about it."

"I'll explain later. I'd better go now. I'll be back soon. They've been waiting for me."

He kissed her quickly and dashed out. Minou looked out of the window into the street. A car stood in the driveway with its engine running. Javad and the other men—there were four—got into it and drove off.

Was the newspaper a part of the "rut" he feared to fall back into? But a momentary expression of pride had lit his face as he was leaving. Minou opened her suitcase and took out a few things—a set of clothes, a nightgown, her toothbrush and comb—the necessities. She was at a loss as to where to put everything in this unfamiliar house, how to divide the space between herself and Javad. His suitcase lay there on the floor, suddenly looking misplaced. That leaden depression kept weighing her down.

She heard a tune coming from the courtyard. She looked out. Ali was sitting in the doorway of his room with his shirt off and his legs crossed under him, playing the flute. She was grateful that he had come along.

She came back and lay on the bed with her clothes on, waiting for Javad. Then midnight was approaching, but he was not back. She put on her nightgown and turned off the light.

Javad was whistling in the shower. Minou was not sure what time he had returned. She had slept heavily, extraordinarily tired from all the recent activities.

She lay there waiting for him to come out of the shower, then she fell asleep again. When she woke she found a note and a pile of newspapers called *Ijtemah* on the table beside the bed. He said, in the note, that he had gone to school to look at his mail and to do some other things he had to get done before registration, which was the following week.

She pulled the curtains open and looked into the sun-filled courtyard. Toads hopped in and out of a flower bed near the window. Her depression had lifted as if dissolved in dreams.

She got dressed and ate her breakfast, which Ali served

to her. He had already learned how to use the new kitchen. She looked through the newspapers. She saw Javad's name listed as editor. This was what had taken him out last night. She glanced through the articles. Many of them were social commentaries. One of them, written by Javad, was about the need for adult education to bring up the level of literacy. She thought she would try to write for the paper also. The idea excited her.

Then the trunks arrived from the wharf and Ali brought them in to her. She began to unpack. One of the trunks contained only things made of cloth. Her mother had neatly folded everything, even the slips and underpants and handkerchiefs. They had a pleasant scent from the potpourri her mother had made herself and put in with them. Minou arranged Javad's clothes in one closet and hers in another. She put away the sheets, pillowcases, towels, a mantel cover (she decided not to use that—it looked out of place in the modern house), a quilt made of exactly a thousand pieces that had been part of Aunt Narghes' own trousseau, two matching embroidered tablecloths with hummingbirds whirring out of a plum tree at their center, from Aunt Mehri.

She opened the other trunks. Silver tea glass holders, a samovar, black engraved stone bowls, a blue plate with arabesque designs. Sohrab had sent her a pearl necklace; Farzin, a pair of copper trays with identical scenes of a group of women dancing and two men playing sitars pressed into them.

Javad had said they did not need any kitchen utensils and furniture since he had collected all that over the years living by himself. Instead her mother had given her jewelry she had bought in the bazaar—five thin gold bracelets that Minou would wear all together, matching ruby earrings and necklace, a matching amethyst ring and

77

bracelet. She unpacked slowly, rubbing her fingers over the rich, slippery texture of things, thinking that this pleasure was due to her marriage.

Javad came home in the afternoon. He approved of where she had put everything, was appreciative of the presents. His mood was serene. She was eager to bring up the newspaper. "I read your article. You never mentioned the newspaper to me before."

He shrugged.

"Maybe I'll write something for it."

He nodded distractedly. "Let's go out. I want to take you around."

A little later they went out. They walked for a while and then took buses to various spots Javad wanted her to see. He showed her the ruins of a mosque with its golden dome still intact, a shirt factory. The trees surrounding the factory were covered with fluffy loose patches of cotton, looking like an old woman's hair. Through an open door she could see workers, men and women, leaning over spools, spinning out yarn. They passed opium poppy fields stretching for miles. He took her to his school. It was almost a duplicate of her school in Ahvāz, with a large blackboard and a portrait of the Shah in each room and a bell hanging on its veranda.

They stopped at the refineries for a few moments. It was sunset and the sky was splashed with color, changing rapidly from deep purple to pink to red. Tanks holding the petroleum stood within a mile of the derricks and pipes. The flame from the refuse burner was a bright orange, almost blending into the sunset. Not far from the fields stood the residential houses for the refinery employees.

"Look at the way oil is coming out of the ground there," he said.

An oil residue trickled out of a cement pipe.

"It contaminates the water, it kills the fish," he said. "It's worse here than in Ahvāz. One day, when we have enough savings, I'd like to go and live in Tehran. You could go to school then, if you want."

"I'd like that."

"I'll finish my doctorate. I was only a year from getting my degree when I dropped out. Then I'll look for another job."

The sky turned dark blue and it was suddenly dusk. Almost simultaneously flames began to rise from the pipes—the excess gas being burned off. It was like sinister fireworks, so many flames dancing against the sky.

"This will go on for hours. Some people come and picnic here. They don't care about the smell," Javad said.

But Minou was dizzy from it and they left. They got home in time to eat the dinner Ali had prepared—fish, rice with dill and lima beans, yogurt, and spinach salad.

After supper they lay on the hammocks on the veranda, watching the fireflies moving among the leaves of the trees and the pattern the stars made against the extremely black and faraway sky. When the mosquitoes became hard to take they went inside and lay on the bed with the lights on. The room at that hour had a mysterious beauty, full of shadows trembling on the walls. With the two windows left open it was breezy, and now that the petroleum odor had subsided, the air was fragrant from the flowers in the courtyard.

Javad told Minou about his father. He could not recall his father's face except from pictures, but he recalled his scent, of tobacco mostly. He had liked to smoke a pipe after every meal. Javad was still haunted by his father's death. Had it really been an accident or was it suicide or murder, a political murder, for instance? Javad had been too young when it occurred for him to question it then. He told her about his mother coming back from a pilgrimage and bringing a present for him, a portrait of Imam Husain. She had hoped Javad would be a religious man, had tried to indoctrinate him. He spoke about his young cousins with whom he used to spend a lot of time, going mountain climbing and hiking together.

He said, "I'd like to have at least one child. Do you want children?"

"One day. I'd like them to look like you, to have your features." Minou traced his mouth, his nose, with her fingers, imagining little children looking like him. Yet a child was an idea far in the future. She was filled with Javad then and had no room for anyone else. "I love you," she said.

He turned over and kissed her. He put his hand under her blouse, caressing her breasts.

"Let me see your breasts in the light." His voice was affectionate.

She took off her blouse and her brassiere and turned around for him to look.

"You have nice breasts."

"They're small."

"I like them like this." He held her breasts in his hands, gently, as if they were fruit he was about to pick from a tree.

She shook a little from excitement. Slowly he removed the rest of her clothes and his own, and for the first time they made love with the light on.

They made love in every corner of the house. She liked the touch of her own skin where Javad had touched, the shape of her own lips as she pressed them on his. His body, the male body, fascinated her, the different dimensions and protuberances, all put there for her to receive. The fact that he had once been unattainable and was now so near still excited her.

On the nights that Ali was out they took off their clothes and dipped themselves in the small pool in the courtyard, which looked enlarged under the vast sky above. Naked, in Javad's embrace, she had an odd sensation of all past pleasures instilling themselves into this one single experience, condensed and shiny. They splashed water on each other. They kissed. Finally they came out and, wrapping towels around themselves, went back inside. They made love, their bodies still a little slippery.

Sometimes they lay on the bed and he read to her, sections of articles he wrote, a story that he had translated. Minou liked one story in particular. It was about a blind man who, after twenty years, regains his eyesight and finds the world so much uglier than his fantasy of it that he commits suicide.

They went to the movies, saw all the foreign ones that came to town. She said to him, "I used to be envious of women in American movies. They seem so free."

"Don't you feel that way now?"

"I feel a little freer now."

"I have rescued you?" He smiled.

"Tell me about other women you've known."

"They're all in the past."

"Do you ever think about their kisses?"

"No."

He did not ask her, she noticed, whom she might have known before him. He was confident that she had never been attracted to anyone else, that her contact with men, if any, had been limited. At the same time she had a hunch that perhaps he, alone among all the men she had ever met, did not attach much importance to it one way or the other, that her purity, which she had been told, over and over, to guard, meant nothing to him.

His slightest rebuff upset her. Once he started going out after dinner. She said, "Where are you going? I'll go with you."

"I'm dropping in at school to get something I need." He went out, but he turned around and came back. He took her hand and said, "Let's go."

She laughed; she had been about to cry before.

Abadan was different in many ways from any other town in Iran. Built by the English all at one time, it had a foreign look to it. Different languages were spoken by people living there. There were No Smoking signs everywhere because of the inflammable oil. There was an Arabic market with imported things from Iraq and Kuwait—silk fabrics, ornate gold and silver jewelry, hand-carved boxes—for sale at great bargains. Scattered on Shatt-al-Arab were small islands, owned by Iraqi sheikhs who had set up tents and houses made of straw.

The house they lived in was small enough for her to manage with Ali's help, and she tried to make it look the best it could. She rearranged some of the furniture, replaced a few things. To the flowers already in bloom in the courtyard she added new ones. With a lot of watering they grew rapidly, particularly dahlias, which shot up in bright colors. Gradually she came to enjoy doing some cooking, though at first it was difficult. The first time she tried to fry something the butter began to sizzle and a few drops splashed against her face. Another time she burned the vegetables she was cooking, filling the house with smoke.

She found enough novelty in these domestic activities. What unexpected pleasure there was in putting various ingredients together and producing a taste different from that of each of the items going into it. She liked making lists for herself and getting the tasks on them accomplished by the end of the day. She walked almost everywhere, with Ali or by herself, only occasionally depending on buses or taxis. She always came across a new shop tucked away in an alley or an interesting-looking house.

Some days she lay on the hammock and listened, hour after hour, to the radio or records on the portable phonograph, or she read. There were always piles of books and magazines, some in English, that Javad kept around to look through for material to translate. The veranda was cool, shaded by a cluster of trees and insulated by stone walls.

From that spot she could see the woman living across the street climbing the ladder to the roof, her *chador* tied around her waist, a ceramic pitcher of water on her shoulder. On the roof the woman set up a mosquito net and spread mattresses inside it. She shook out a rug, hung the clothes she had washed on ropes. She had seen the woman on the street several times, pushing an older woman on a cart. The old woman sat still with her *chador* wrapped around her as if she were a doll. Minou had talked with the young woman once. She said her name was Zohreh and the older woman was her mother. The old woman could

no longer walk because of severe arthritis. In an over-
familiar tone Zohreh went on to say, "We were all happy
to see Javad *khan* coming back here married. We tried to
think of a girl who might be suitable for him. There were
several eligible ones, but he was aloof, and we left him
alone." Minou did not pursue the conversation. Zohreh
was making her uncomfortable.

Minou's days, with their slow rhythm, were mainly
punctuated by Javad coming and going. Javad leaving for
school and returning. Someone knocking on the door and
his running out, his meeting with the four men who col-
laborated with him on *Ijtemah*. He had promised he
would try to convince the other editors to include Minou
on the paper, but so far there was no decision. He explained they had agreed at some point to keep out wives,
cousins, friends. At the beginning they had brought in
others and it had resulted in chaos. He hoped, though, to
talk them eventually into making an exception for her.

Ijtemah came out monthly. Javad and the other four
men wrote the articles and edited them. They had the
paper printed by a man they knew who did it inexpen-
sively. Their main goal was to expose people to certain issues that were normally kept out of other, commercial
newspapers. *Ijtemah* had its origin in informal gatherings
Javad and the other men used to have. They would get
together in one of their houses, drink, and discuss articles
they read. The discussions often became feverish,
obsessive, keeping them up all night. They called their
group the "Secret Circle," as the issues with which they
concerned themselves often had political overtones. It was
Javad who brought up the idea of putting the result of
these talks into a coherent form. He had been inspired by a
sight he had encountered on the Square. Sitting aimlessly
on a bench, he had seen a man lying under the canopy of a

store across the street. The man kept twisting his body as though in agony. Then he suddenly collapsed on the ground. He seemed to be under the influence of a drug. So many people in Abadan took opium and heroin. Javad started to go toward him but stopped halfway. He simply did not have the motivation. Or was it something else that stopped him, a sense of helplessness? Other people collected around the man and finally he was taken away. Later, Javad was devastated by his own paralysis. He kept thinking of a way that he might make a dent, however small, in what went on around him.

At first they were more daring in what they wrote in the paper. In one article they had mentioned that the per capita income of farmers in Iran for a month was less than the per capita income of an American farmer for a day. And they blamed this on the Ministry of Agriculture. One of the editors, Asghar, a teacher from another high school, went to jail because of this. It was arbitrary that it was he rather than Javad or any of the others. At the beginning of Asghar's prison term no one was allowed to go and visit him, but finally they gained permission to see him once. Javad visited him in his windowless cell. Asghar had lost weight and his skin had an unhealthy sallowness. He said he had been tortured with electric shocks. He came out after a year, a different person, full of bitterness. Since then they had avoided direct political statements in the newspaper. But Javad said, "We don't want to always live with these restrictions, in this cowardly manner. Sooner or later there will have to be a breakthrough for us."

Minou recalled having seen the courtyard of a jail from the roof of a public building. Two men in drab beige clothes and with shaved heads were sweeping dry leaves into a garbage bag. A group of men sat in a corner picking out husks from grains of rice spread on a tray.

She also recalled accompanying her father into a

women's penitentiary, where he was going to see one of his clients. They had been out on another errand first. Minou could not have been more than seven or eight years old. She had sat in the waiting room while her father disappeared inside. A space heater gave out inadequate heat and the air had a sour smell like spoiled milk. Intermittently there were sounds of weeping from somewhere inside.

A woman, her face streaming with tears, came into the room and sat across from Minou. She was followed by another woman and a little girl. They were all wearing *chadors*. The little girl started to cry, her face contorted with fear.

Outside, Minou's father said to her, "That's what happens when you disobey the law, you get locked up like an animal in a cage." Her father was stirred up.

When the editors met in their house their conversation sounded like a commotion to Minou, full of urgency. They spoke about the deaths in the oil fields, workers who died of heatstroke, many of them working long hours in the unrelenting sun, about introducing better books to students at schools, about the disconcertingly high degree of illiteracy in the country. Sometimes they sat in the courtyard under lanterns hanging from a tree, their silhouettes mysterious in that light. Often after these meetings Javad had a hard time sleeping and he got out of the bed and read or used the time to work on his translation or an article for the next issue of the paper. He wrote many pages, pouring out everything about a point he wanted to make, then edited them to size. He wrote longhand in a thick notebook he kept on his desk and then had his notes typed by someone on the Square.

One of the members of *Ijtemah*, Jamal, a poet by profession, invited everyone, including the wives, to lunch at his house. He lived in an out-of-the-way neighborhood. The house was tucked at the end of a narrow alley, off a winding street. The living room was furnished with rugs and cushions and brass lanterns. They sat against cushions in the cavernous, windowless room, the women slightly separate from the men. They had fruit and nuts, beer and *sharbat,* which a servant brought over to them, and they talked. All the men—Javad; Jamal; Asghar; Hassan, an architect; and Parviz, a lawyer—were informally dressed. They had an intellectual air and manner. Asghar wore tight-fitting clothes and sunglasses although they were indoors. He spoke little and very softly. When he did speak, everyone listened carefully. Parviz was large and robust and rather loud. Sometimes he jumped up with excitement. The other two men were more ordinary in their bearing. They talked about abstract issues—what would improve a society, how a city could be built to best accommodate its citizens.

The women were more formally dressed—in high heels, silk and jersey dresses, and a lot of makeup. Minou was aware of them judging her, judging one another. Hadn't Asghar's wife plucked her eyebrows too thin, wasn't Hassan's wife wearing too much rouge, and Minou too little of anything? their eyes reflected. Much of their talk was about clothes.

"Your blouse is very pretty."

"May I offer it to you?"

"No, thank you. I was just admiring it."

"Where did you buy that pretty scarf?"

"From Elli, it's English. They carry a lot of nice things."

"Jones is a nice shop, too."

"So many shops have been opening up in the last two years or so. Some life is being blown into Abadan finally."

They drifted onto other subjects.

"They found a dead body this morning in the river—a fisherman pulled it out. I heard it on the radio."

"That tall man living with his mother at the corner of our street was taken away in the middle of the night last week on some charge."

"Probably he did some antigovernment things."

"He's never going to come back."

"His mother was crying by the door of their house."

"He shouldn't have gotten involved in that kind of thing."

"Some of these young men ask for trouble."

"Maybe it's worth it for them."

Asghar's wife, Simin, suddenly looked dispirited. Was she thinking of her husband's period in jail?

Minou was not really participating in the conversation. They all knew one another so well. She was filled with longing for her friends in Ahvāz. She had a sudden feeling of disorientation as though landing from a height. She envied Javad for his sense of involvement with the men, which went beyond friendship, was partly sparked by their deeply shared interest in *Ijtemah.* Her desire to work on the paper was renewed again. Had Javad really tried hard enough to convince the other editors to include her?

Other sounds mingled with the voices—the buzzing of flies, hammering from a welding shop, the hum of vendors on the street, a muezzin calling people to prayers.

Then everyone stopped talking as Jamal began to play his lute. He played and recited, with half-shut eyes, poems which, Simin told Minou, he had written himself.

> *The thought of all those*
> *In slumber makes me want to shout.*
> *They sleep at night, they sleep in*
>   *daylight,*
> *The sun, with all its glitter, blinding*
>   *them.*

And:

We are a land of dreamers,
Deep in a trance from which we
Rarely come out.
Our reality is too bitter to face
  awake.

The servant came in and spread a cloth on the floor and arranged dishes on it for lunch. Then he brought out the food. Jamal stopped, although everyone asked him to go on awhile longer. They began to eat. When they were finished, the servant cleared away the dishes and the cloth and brought over tea. After a while the men began to play backgammon and the women talked among themselves again.

Finally it was time to go and there was the chorus of farewells, with Jamal insisting that they were all leaving too early and that next time they should stay longer, while the guests said they had already troubled him enough.

On the way home Minou said to Javad, "It was a different kind of a day from what I expected."

"What did you expect?" He seemed a little surprised.

"I thought we would all mingle better—men and women."

"The men know each other better."

They talked a little about everyone there. He agreed with her that Asghar had a mysterious air, something which, he said, had not been there before his jail term. He thought Simin was intelligent but somewhat uninvolved with his concerns. He thought that was true about the other wives as well—they were placid, unaffected by what went on around them.

"They aren't given the opportunity to get involved,"

Minou said. "You spend so much time on the paper and yet none of us are allowed to have a part in it."

"I see what you mean."

"I could try one article and you show it to them. If. . ."

"That's not the point, whether you write well or not. We had promised to keep the paper only to the five of us, or else everyone has a cousin or a niece."

"You didn't even mention the possibility to them?"

"I hinted at it a couple of times. No one seemed open to it." He looked a little meditative, then he said, "Why don't you write some stories as you did in my class? I'll read them. Isn't that enough?"

She shook her head. All the action and excitement of his life revolved around the newspaper.

The sense of disappointment lingered with her all the way home. She complained, "You're always busy with your work while I just sit home."

He pulled her to his chest and said, "Are you feeling sorry for yourself?" He caressed her hair, her buttocks. "My work has its limitations. We have to be cautious all the time, as you know." He kissed her over and over as though to compensate for other lacks. His mouth still on her lips, he unzipped the back of her dress and, pulling off the straps, let the dress fall. He took off her brassiere, her pants. In a moment the two of them lay in bed, and he was kissing her everywhere. She shuddered with desire, writhed under his touch. He undressed himself. Every part of their bodies interlocked.

It was hard at that moment not to relinquish despair.

As she was leaving Ahvāz, on the wharf, her mother had said to her, "You poor thing, you're going to be all alone."

"I will be with Javad, and with Ali, too, for a while." But she knew what her mother meant: that Minou would not have another woman to confide in, the soft touch of a woman, her sympathetic ears.

Now she complained to her mother on the phone. Her mother asked her to come home for a visit.

"Why don't you come here? You haven't seen my house yet," she said tentatively. She was not sure she wanted her parents to visit yet. Her mother would inspect every part of her house, every aspect of her life, and find faults, give advice on improvement. Her father would be stiff, pontificate, look bored out of his own environment.

"I will, as soon as I can. You know your father doesn't like me to leave him alone," her mother said, perhaps responding to her reservations. Minou had discouraged her from coming with her at the beginning, when she just moved there.

"Come with him," she said in the same tentative tone.

"He's working every day and likes to spend Fridays with his friends. Do you want your Aunt Narghes to come over?"

"No, it's all right. I'll manage."

"Can I send you anything?"

"No, no, I have everything."

Still her mother sent her packages of food and clothing as if Minou were far away in a primitive village.

She did not encourage a visit from Javad's mother for the same reason. His mother would try to run her days, ask her questions she was not ready to answer.

She was afraid to be engulfed by them before she had found her own way.

Some evenings she and Ali went to the wharf and looked at the ships that came from all over the world, their lights winking. It was always crowded with people going away to visit relatives, to attend a wedding or a funeral. They carried bundles, little pillows for their children to rest their heads on. Gaudily dressed, hardened-looking women stood by, laughing loudly and vulgarly, drawing attention to themselves. One would be approached by a sailor and then the two of them would disappear from the wharf into a back street. The sun sank into the sea, distant minarets and domes turned gray and colorless. The stars came out one by one.

On some evenings she read to Ali from the thick leather-bound book he had had for years and of which he knew sections by heart. They sat on a kilim Ali spread on the veranda in front of his room. The parakeet he had bought squawked or shrieked, "Salaam," at regular intervals.

Ali sat cross-legged, his eyes half-shut, coming alive at high points of the story, making an exclamatory remark at the hero's adventures in his search for his beloved who was locked away in a castle. They rarely went into Ali's room, which was small and windowless and cluttered with items he had collected since he came there—he had showed her a water pipe with an emerald-green top he had bought on the Square.

He told Minou about his past. "Before I came to work for your parents I was engaged to a beautiful girl from my village. She was thirteen and at the prime of womanhood, but she was snatched away from me by a richer man, a rug merchant. I was about thirty then. After that I gave up the idea of marrying. Why bother, why start headaches?"

Once late at night, soon after his disappointment, he had come out into the street to direct the gutter water into the pool in his uncle's yard. He put a few large stones into the gutter and watched triumphantly as the water changed direction and entered the pipe leading to the pool. The clear drinking water ran through the gutters only once a week and often caused stiff competition among the inhabitants of the district. From a distance he could see some figures standing together, engaged in the same task as he. The hum of their voices barely reached him in the windless night.

Then he saw the light of a kerosine lamp moving toward him, and from behind it appeared the young merchant. He had a long stick in his hand and, bending low, he pushed it against the stones in the water. They collapsed in a heap, dispersing the water from its small canal. Ali told him he had no right to do that. The merchant said Ali was a no-body, whereas everyone knew him, he was of a good family. Ali and the man began to grapple with each other. Ali managed to bring the man down to the ground. He sat on him and would not let go until the man apologized. That softened the edge of the other defeat that Ali had suffered over the girl.

He regretted his lack of education. When he was a child the village he had lived in caught fire and burned down completely. He and his family went to live in another village. An earthquake destroyed that, too. Both his parents died in the earthquake. After that he lived with differ-ent relatives. In one of the bedrooms of his childhood there was a framed picture of a battlefield on the wall. It was in-scribed underneath with ornate, gold letters that sparkled with mystery in sunlight. He gazed at them, trying to decipher their meaning. Perhaps they held a truth that would enlighten the dim path before him. He had often looked at these letters, but then he felt strangled with an-guish because he could not read, because he would go on for the rest of his life ignorant of a vast dimension of knowledge. He came to the window and looked at the leaves, which were translucent like jade in sunlight, at the yellow pollen floating in the air. Some inner light had van-ished from them. Their poetry was destroyed. They were counterfeit. He looked again at the letters on the wall. They winked at him like valuable jewels.

At that time he worked in a bakery. He stood by the flaming furnace throwing in triangular lumps of dough. The customers were mostly servants and children, but occasionally a lawyer, a doctor, a teacher came in. He had noticed the respect with which these customers were treated by the owner—his eyes would shine with an ingratiating spark, his voice became servile, and he served them before their turn.

One night Ali lay in his bed with the sound of the word "school" enveloping him like a soft, feathery blanket. He whispered the word over and over until it took on shape, shining before him in the dark. The next day, he decided, he would talk to his uncle and beg him to let him go to school. But, as fate had it, a flood occurred and once again they had to move. His uncle became destitute.

"There's only one door open to us." He thought about that and added, "It's our fate whether we can enter it or not."

Tears were glistening in his eyes, sad on his old, lined faced. Minou wished she could do something for him, to wipe out years of disappointment and suffering, but all she could do was stare at him helplessly.

12

One evening Minou persuaded Javad to take time off from work and see *Diary of a Mad Housewife*, an American movie that had first been banned for being "immoral" because a part of its plot had to do with marital infidelity. Then it had been cut somewhat and allowed to be shown. The movie had been drawing crowds for days.

He was a little late and they dashed out, taking a taxi over to the noisy, crowded, well-lit Meli Street, where the cinema stood next to a row of glittering buildings. Boys stood under streetlights and stared at girls going by. Fashionable men and women, many of them speaking foreign languages, strolled by. Some paused and studied the billboards of the cinema, the shop windows with their displays of cards, records, radios, imported watches, and perfumes. Music blared out of shops, cars zoomed by. There was a lively, shiny look to the whole street, but the bright façade hid forbidden things, gambling, prostitution. In the dark shadows of doorways local hoodlums stood in clusters, cajoling people to buy cigarettes (which Javad said was a code for opium). Above the gymnasium, there was a "pleasure house." Young girls from the villages, lured by the luxury promised them, worked there as stripteasers. The street was a more extreme version of Pahlavi Street in Ahvāz.

Inside the cinema the lights were already turned off and they had to walk slowly, guided by the usher's flashlight. Most of the seats were taken. They sat close to the screen. He held her hand in his, squeezing it gently.

The movie was light entertainment but with very good acting, Minou thought. Halfway through it Minou became aware of a gray layer hanging high in the air. The images on the screen became hazy. The air had a smoky smell. There was a cough and then another. She and Javad also started coughing. Heads kept turning around. Minou could feel her breathing become difficult.

"What's going on?" someone said. "It's so smoky here."

"We'd better get out of here," Javad said. "It looks like there's a fire somewhere."

They got up and started for one of the exit doors. They could see a tiny flame rising and falling in the projection window, a bright, greedy tongue moving toward them. Smoke swirled around the flame. "There it is," Javad said.

"A fire," a man said loudly.

"Fire!" said another man.

Several people began to run toward the exit doors.

Javad tried to open the door, but it seemed to be locked from the outside. "Why is this door locked?" he said.

Several men joined in, struggling to open the door.

"Why have they locked us in?" a man said.

Quickly the place was in chaos, with everyone standing behind the doors and banging on them or shouting.

"Why is this locked?"

"Are they trying to kill us?"

"Help, help!"

"Fire!"

"Fire!"

"Why isn't anyone helping us?"

"I'm suffocating."

"This is hell."

A baby began to cry in a shrill, frightened way.

"Someone ought to do something!"

"I'm afraid."

"This way," Javad said, grabbing Minou's hand and running behind the screen. "Maybe there's another door here."

There was no door, but there was a small window. Javad pulled at the latch—it came open.

He picked her up and she squeezed herself out. The window was reasonably close to the ground, but Minou realized once she landed that she would have jumped from any height.

Javad was shouting to the others inside, "There's a window here." Then he climbed up and squeezed with even more difficulty out of the window onto the street. She saw him jumping out through black smoke.

Smoke was filling the street. They both kept coughing. People were coming out of the window, coughing. A woman's *chador* caught in the window as she jumped out. She shrieked, "My God, my God," ripped her *chador* from the window, and quickly put it on, looking humiliated.

"I hope someone has reported this," Javad said.

"I'm going to the police station," another man said. "I have a car right here."

"Yes, in case no one else has," Javad said. He went to the window and tried to help people climb out. Minou joined him. A woman was crying as she held on to Javad's hands. As soon as she landed on the ground she began to throw up, soiling the front of her dress. Javad gave her a handkerchief. A woman lifted her child to the window and asked Javad to take him. The child was crying loudly. The mother climbed up herself and jumped out. A young boy jumped out, and then he began to run, shouting, "Fire, fire!"

The whole street was becoming congested with automobiles and people. Everyone kept asking, "What's happening, what's going on?"

"The fire engines should have been here by now. What's taking them so long?" a man said.

"There is no sign of the ushers or the manager," another man said.

"They must have gone to get help. Calling these places takes forever."

"Why are the doors locked?"

A woman was trying to climb up the window and was having a hard time. Javad and Minou kept pulling her hands and she kept falling back down. Finally they managed to pull her up. She climbed over Javad's shoulders and then jumped down to the ground. "I'm afraid of heights," she said through her coughing.

Minou's lungs were filling with smoke. She started to vomit. "I can't stand here any longer," she said, wiping her mouth with her handkerchief.

"I'm getting sick myself," Javad said.

They could hear sirens, then the fire engine's red lights whirred in the air. A cry of relief rose from the crowd. Firemen, carrying ladders and other equipment, dashed out of trucks.

Minou wished she could stay and watch, but she was faint and very nauseous. "We'd better go."

They began to walk home, looking back frequently. Thin flames embedded in black smoke were rising from the roof of the cinema. Javad kept pausing and listening, as though he expected to be called back. Minou was beginning to have a floating feeling from inhaling the fresh air.

At home they drank several glasses of water. They washed, undressed, and got into bed. There were scratch marks on their arms from scraping against the window, but nothing serious. Then they lay there and listened to the radio for the news of the fire. The scene kept passing before Minou's eyes like a vision in a dream, people jumping out one by one through the smoky window, the panic on the faces, shouts.

All the stations were covering news about the government's land reform plan, how each peasant was going to get a share of land, which would be taken away from the landlords by the government. Nothing about the fire yet.

The next day the fire was in the headlines of all the local newspapers and on the radio stations.
Abadan News said:

There was a fire last night around 8:30 at the Zenith Cinema, where *Diary of a Mad Housewife* was being shown, killing forty people and injuring many others. The fire apparently started in the projection room during the movie and got out of hand. It seems to have been started by a cigarette falling onto a pile of paper. Mr. Parviz Poorani, the projectionist, must have put a half-finished cigarette in an ashtray on the table next to him. The police speculated that he could have fallen asleep. He was among the forty who died in the fire. According to officials, the deaths were mostly caused by panic. Otherwise everyone would have been able to get out of the cinema's back window, used by those who did escape. Those injured in the rush were taken to the Refinery Hospital. The men we spoke with were bewildered, not knowing exactly what happened. They only recalled rushing to the doors and finding them locked. The twenty men in the hospital are in fair condition.

Even the staff did not act calmly. They had all dashed out as soon as they became aware of the fire and run to the nearby police and fire stations. We spoke to Mr. Sahib, one of the managers. He said his staff had been afraid a phone call or waiting for a taxi would take longer than walking. Unfortunately, in their panic, they neglected to unlock the doors before they left. The fire trucks arrived too late to rescue everyone. It took several hours to put out the fire, which spread rapidly to different parts of the building. The frame of the building, however, has remained intact. . . .

There were photographs of the fire at its late stages, when the flames seemed to be consuming every piece of the cinema, and dark shapes of firemen working on the rooftop.

The fire had become the main topic of discussion everywhere. There was a hint of doom in the tone. The concern was almost mystical in its intensity.

There were different theories about how the fire might have started: that the owners of the cinema had started it to collect insurance money, that it was the work of one crazy person, that the government had, for unknown reasons, a part in it—maybe its intention was to murder several specific persons attending the movie (and that was why the doors were kept locked)—and it had bribed the staff to cooperate. Javad believed that it was the work of a fanatic religious group, Bandeh Khoda, men who opposed all movies on moral grounds.

In the afternoon Minou and Javad went to look at the

sight. The building was black, the billboards practically all destroyed. A part of the roof had collapsed, and so had the wooden frames of the windows and the entire front door. The tops of the palm trees around the cinema were scorched. There were smoke marks on the sides of the near-by buildings, as if sooty hands had touched them randomly. Men were carrying out equipment and putting it into a truck. As on the night before, the street was crowded with traffic and people looking on. Reporters walked around the building, taking pictures. Javad was scribbling down some notes on a sheet of paper. He was planning to write an article on the fire.

Several men, women, and children, presumably relatives of the dead, were wailing. One woman said, between sobs, "You're going to pay for this, murderers, if not in this world, then in the next."

A man standing next to Minou and Javad whispered, "They shouldn't have gone to see the movie to begin with."

Another man said, "Yes, it's God's punishment."

"If we don't watch out we're all going to burn alive."

"The movies are the least of the evils. Think of all the clubs sprouting with half-naked foreign girls dancing in them. They get them young and fresh from Europe and America. They let the higher officials have their pick first and then some of the lower-downs have their choices. Finally they are dumped into the nightclubs for the common man."

"That's the kind of filth I hope to see wiped out. It's disgraceful to see sin infesting our country."

"Some of them have gonorrhea and syphilis even though they look shining clean."

"Sure, they're like any prostitute. How they tempt us men! They know all sorts of tricks, I've heard, young as some of them are."

"I wouldn't go near one. What if I did catch a disease? They should lock up women like that behind bars and put a sack over their heads."

"Our country has become a crazy place."

"The clubs, the gambling halls, these filthy movies—let them all burn, why not?"

"All the evil of money, the dollar. Our young men think they've conquered the world if they have a big, shiny American car to ride around in."

Three blond men were standing on the other side of the street, inspecting the sight, taking pictures like the other reporters.

"Look at them, don't they act pompous? It's as if they own this town. Our government pays them four times better than our own workers in equivalent positions. They live in much better houses, have access to summer places and chauffeur-driven cars. They laugh at us behind our backs. They have no respect for our ways of doing things."

"Yes, they know one thing, money."

"They steal the oil money that should go into improving the lives of the poor and spend it on their corrupt pleasures."

The voices were drowned by cars honking, each driver trying to pass the others.

What would Abadan, a hot, petroleum-choked town, be like without these sources of escape? Minou wondered. The movies were glimpses of possibilities of a freedom for which she had craved all her life.

From what she could see, the inside of the cinema was completely vacated, looking like an empty tomb.

Then two uniformed policemen came out of the side door, carrying a body wrapped in a white sheet. The sheet was pushed aside a little as the policemen tried to put the body in the back seat of their car. Minou had a glimpse of the dead person's face. It was burned so much that it was hard to know whether it belonged to a man or a woman. A pang of terror went through Minou as she stared. There was no hair on the head, one eye socket was empty, and the skin was charred like a piece of wood.

"My God," she heard Javad saying. He was shaking his head.

They stood there for a long time, repelled by and drawn to the sight at the same time.

Javad spent the next few afternoons and evenings working on the article, mostly interviewing people, trying to arrive at his own conclusion about the cause of the fire and the number of deaths. Minou asked if she could go with him, but he said it would be difficult—a woman's presence would prevent some people from speaking freely. Minou was aware of a wave of frustration again because she could not participate in the newspaper.

Minou did something she had not done before. She called Simin, Asghar's wife, to talk to her about the fire. Simin had seemed the most open of all the editors' wives when Minou met the group.

"I'm tired of the newspaper. It has left no life for me and Asghar together. He's gone all the time."

"I wish there was a way we could get involved."

"I'm not sure I want that. I could live without all the headaches. I just hope they aren't endangering themselves. People are put in jail for the slightest thing." In a confidential tone she added, "Asghar was in jail already, for a year, over something he wrote."

"Javad told me about it. He said after that they stopped taking chances."

"It was a nightmare." She invited Minou to tea.

Her house, as well as her appearance this time, was unexpected. The house was old and decaying, with musty-smelling hallways, a weed-choked courtyard, a chipped stairway leading to the roof. The living room was untidy, cluttered with diapers, baby clothes, an overturned kettle. The furniture was battered. On the day of the party Simin had been dressed up in a silk blouse and skirt and high-heeled patent-leather shoes, her hair perfectly combed into place, her makeup and nail polish flawless. Today her dress was stained with food, her lipstick, left from the night before, cracked, her nail polish peeling.

During the short time Minou was visiting, Simin moved around in a fluttery manner, distracted by her two young boys, one nine months and the other two and a half years old. The infant kept pushing the pacifier out of his mouth and crying, tensing his muscles. "There's nothing wrong with you and you know it," Simin said to him in a half-affectionate, half-scolding tone. She served Minou tea, holding the baby in one arm over her hip.

Her older boy kept touching the breakable objects, and she had to watch him constantly. Then he pulled down a ceramic flowerpot from the mantel. Some of the dirt fell on his face and chest. He began to cry. Simin picked up the pot and then excused herself to go and clean up the boy's face. She asked Minou to take care of the baby for a few moments. Minou sipped at her tea and watched the baby on the couch. Simin came back, looking a little ashamed. She began to have her tea and said, "I had three miscarriages before Jafaar was born. We're grateful to have these two."

Before Minou had a chance to reply Simin jumped up. Jafaar had picked up a marble and was putting it into his mouth. "You're old enough not to do this," she snapped.

In spite of all the commotion between her and her children there was something stationary and weighed down about the house, Minou thought. Simin, out of her fashionable clothes, was bedraggled and bewildered by her domestic chores and at the same time, in an odd way, accepting of them.

Finally Minou left, without having discussed all the things she was aching to talk about.

The fire was the headline of the next *Ijtemah* issue. "One hundred and fifty died in the fire." The essence of the article was: "...There has been such a huge distortion about the number of deaths in the fire and we have been led to believe the cause of the fire might also be falsified. The facts are that the fire was reported too late, the two exit doors were locked, perhaps kept locked, and there were no signs of the ushers or the managers at the time of the fire. Some investigations support our suspicions that the group calling itself Bandeh Khoda, opposing movies, and in particular *Diary of a Mad Housewife*, might have played a part in starting the fire...."

They rushed the paper to the printers and got it on the newsstands within three days. That evening Minou and Javad went out to a restaurant. They returned late at night to a disturbing sight. Stacks and stacks of *Ijtemah* lay on the front steps of their house. Some of them were torn into parts, others muddied so that they could not be salvaged. They were like corpses thrown on their doorway. They would not disappear by a blink of an eye.

"I can't believe this," Javad said. "These must be practically all the copies." His voice shook a little.

"After all that work. Who could possibly have done this?"

"Obviously someone who's angry about the fire article. Let's take them inside," he said.

Silent, dispirited, they picked up the papers and took them to his study. Then they sat across from each other, locked in mutual despair. Javad's face was drained of color.

"Tomorrow tell Ali to dispose of these. There's no point in keeping them around," he said.

Finally he got on the phone and told Jamal what had happened. His words were bitter and angry.

Suddenly Minou was afraid for Javad. There was news weekly of people simply disappearing or being arrested on a minor charge and put in jail. Someone was angry at him about the article and could harm him.

She got up and went into the bedroom, undressing. She heard him coming in and then felt his hands caressing her arms, her breasts. She was startled by his touch in the mood they were in. His hands circled around and around her breasts.

They lay in bed and made love more forcefully than ever before. Their bodies moved into one another like some fluid substance, merging, becoming one. But when he pulled back, and each solidified again, he became lost to her, too sharply delineated. It upset her how he totally withdrew from her. There was a space around him into which she was not allowed to enter, a cold, dark vista. It was hard to quite pin it down, but it was as if all her fervor, the act of lovemaking, had crystallized into a little ball and rolled away, taking with it the essence of what had a moment ago united them. She lay there, acutely lonely.

13

The word had nevertheless gotten around about the article. Javad received several letters commending him for his courage or threatening him for printing lies. There were a few letters from the families of those who had died, pouring out their grief over the accident, cursing whoever might have been responsible for the fire. One mother wrote that she was going to complain to government officials. None of the names on the letters were familiar to Javad.

The phone would not stop ringing.

Javad said to Minou, "You answer it next time, tell them I'm not in."

But one man was persistent. He said, "Are you sure? Tell him this is Rahman."

Minou turned to Javad and, covering the receiver with her hand, said, "He says to tell you it's Rahman."

Javad sat on the edge of the bed and talked to the man for a long time. Minou could see that he was distressed. He crumpled up a piece of paper lying on the table and tapped his foot against the bed.

"I'm flattered you like it. You're right, I should have checked with you. You'd know the facts better than anybody. . . . I don't see any point to it. . . . If you really think so. . . You're right. . . . Yes, I'll come tonight, with Minou. . . ."

He put the receiver down and got up.

"What was that about?" Minou asked.

"It was an old friend. He's a doctor, works at the Refinery Hospital. He had read the article about the fire and wanted to tell me he liked it. He invited us to go to their house tonight."

"I'd like that." Minou was eager to meet new people.

In an hour they began to get ready. She looked through her clothes for something that would be flattering. She settled on a white and yellow cotton dress and a pair of dangling gold earrings.

"How do I look?"

"Fine, fine." He glanced at her quickly. He had only changed his shirt.

Javad was quiet on the bus going over, preoccupied. They got out in the residential section of the refineries. One street was lined entirely by Western-style houses, their grass-covered backyards separated from one another by short fences. The gas lamps on the doors formed little pools of yellow light.

"That's their house," Javad said, pointing to a large, semimodern house with tall trees showing above a fence surrounding its yard.

They walked down the gravel path and he rang the bell.

A man opened the door. "Javad," he said excitedly. The two of them embraced.

They drew apart and Javad said, "This is Minou."

The man nodded at her. "I'm Rahman. My wife and I have been eager to meet you. Come in, come in."

They went through a rug-covered corridor into the living room.

A woman was sitting on the sofa. "I'm glad Rahman persuaded you to come," she said to Javad, getting up. There was a moment of awkwardness between her and Javad, a kind of avoidance of the eyes.

Javad introduced them. The woman's name was Pari. She nodded at Minou and then turned quickly to Javad again. "There aren't that many worthwhile people in Abadan. One can't forget about those few there are."

They all sat down. Rahman asked them if they wanted anything to drink. He turned to Minou. "Do you drink?"

"A little."

Everyone asked for wine.

Rahman went to the cabinet in a corner, took out a bottle of wine and glasses, and brought them over. He put them on the table next to platters of pistachio nuts, almonds, and halvah already set there. The glasses were crystal, the plates gold-rimmed. Everything in the room seemed expensive. Original miniature paintings hung on the walls, a silk rug covered the floor. A cabinet with arabesque designs carved into it stood in a corner. Lamps with pink shades gave the room a pleasant rosy glow. Jasmine blossoms floated on the water in a ceramic bowl set in the middle of the table. They moved slowly with the breeze from the window, meeting and separating again.

"You really abandoned us," Rahman said.

"I've mainly been working."

An awkward silence followed.

Rahman took a quick gulp of his wine. "I can use this. I just came back from the hospital. People come in with heatstroke. At least half of them die. They can't be helped."

"I couldn't take being a nurse for that very reason," Pari said. "Even two years of it was too long."

"You've found something to do with yourself," Javad said. He turned to Minou. "Pari designed the patterns on that tablecloth."

Minou looked at the geometric design. "That's very nice."

"By the way, I attended to three of the men burned in the fire. They were in deep shock when they were brought in. None of them recovered," Rahman remarked.

"Minou and I were in the cinema when the fire started."

"That must have been some scene. But you managed to get out."

"It didn't seem that bad at the time," Minou said.

"We climbed out the back window. That was the only way out," Javad said. He went on to describe it.

"It's incredible that help came so late," Rahman said. "On the other hand, everything is inefficient in Abadan. Where did you get your figures?"

"From friends and relatives. Still, I'm sure they're more accurate than the official figures."

"I think so."

"Why is it that we're so dominated by the few at the top? Why this terrible oppression?" Javad asked.

"Its roots are in poverty, scarcity."

"We don't need to be poor—we have all the resources, oil, minerals. I think it has more to do with illiteracy. The masses of people are uneducated, so they put their trust in those few who bully them."

Pari was looking at Javad intently. She said, "I agree with you that Bandeh Khoda people must have played a part in the fire. They have been agitating against all the Western influence in Abadan."

"Someone collected the copies of *Ijtemah* and stacked them in front of our house," Minou said, addressing Pari for the first time.

Pari did not respond. She was still looking at Javad.

Javad said, "Very few copies could have been sold before they were collected and thrown into our doorway."

"You're serious? That sounds awful," Pari said.

"That's incredible, very upsetting," Rahman said.

"Do you know that your brother, Karim, came to my school to talk to the principal about introducing religious instruction classes?" Javad said to Rahman.

"I haven't been talking to him lately. As you know, we aren't close the way we used to be. He still wants to play the older brother role with me. I guess I've failed him somehow."

Pari looked agitated. "Karim is a fanatic."

"What's the use of labeling him? He likes to spend his time on what he considers to be a matter of conscience," Rahman said.

"You're being kind," Pari said.

Rahman picked up the bottle of wine and refilled the glasses. He raised his glass into the air and said, "To our friendship." Then he drank the wine in a few gulps.

Pari turned to Javad. "Remember our first few months in Abadan? The three of us were like children in an amusement park, running around and doing things all the time."

"The place was new to us then," Javad said.

"We were excited about things," Rahman said.

"Sometimes we stayed up until dawn, talking," Javad said, catching his friends' wistfulness.

"You were the most energetic of all of us," Pari said.

Minou shifted on the soft, fat sofa with its beige corduroy cover, feeling miserable and lost again as she had when they visited Javad's other friends. She wanted to impress Pari, but she was afraid to say anything lest she reveal herself as a child, as she felt herself to be by comparison. She was silent, observant, and she thought she noticed something that perhaps was meant to be hidden, the tension between Javad and Pari.

Pari was more interesting-looking than beautiful: ivory skin, densely black eyes with little white showing around the large irises, and thick, black hair, cut to the nape of her neck. Rahman was handsome but seemed dry and very self-possessed. Both he and Pari looked about the same age as Javad, in their thirties.

Pari's expression when she looked at Minou fluctuated between haughtiness and cool offhandedness, a contrast to the open affection she directed toward Javad. She had a vague, critical attitude toward Rahman, but on the other hand there was an impression of an underlying dependency between them.

Minou was glad to finally hear Javad saying, "It's getting late. We'd better leave." She wished to be out on the street, in the fresh air.

"Why rush?" Rahman protested.

"Why don't you stay a little longer?" Pari said.

"I still have some work to do tonight for school." Javad got up and the others also rose.

"Let me drive you home," Rahman said.

"No thanks, that isn't necessary. We'll take the bus or a taxi."

"This time don't stay away for so long," Pari said. "Now that you're here, I realize how much I've missed our friendship."

Javad embraced her and then Rahman quickly. Then they all said good-bye and left.

Minou walked quietly alongside Javad to the bus stop. They had lost each other in the company of people he had known intimately and for whom he clearly still had strong feelings. The sense of having been excluded lingered with her. There had been such obvious attraction between him and Pari.

She could not quite digest her own reactions. The conflict of her feelings for Pari seemed to have deeper roots than mere jealousy of Javad's attention to her. Although Pari's educated way of speaking and dressing was everything that Minou wanted for herself, as this ideal was presented to her, personified in Pari, she hated it.

Finally Javad asked, "Did you like Pari and Rahman?"

"I don't know," she said moodily.

"Were you bored? You must have been. You could have tried to enter the conversation a little more."

"How could I? You knew each other so well."

What he said next surprised her. "Don't worry. We won't see them again."

But he was clearly stirred up by the visit. She woke several times in the night to his tossing and turning.

In the morning she said, "They obviously meant so much to you. What happened?"

"We just drifted apart. There were little tensions that never got settled." He paused and then said, "Rahman is a bitter man, a little disillusioned with his profession, all the hopeless cases he sees mostly created by ignorance and poverty."

"Was he ever a part of your 'Secret Circle'?"

"No, he chose not to be. He likes to spend all his time on his work." He tapped her arm. "Have I told you enough?"

She felt like an intruder again, as she had the night before.

As he was leaving the house he said, "We lead such stupid, such dull lives here. I'm in my thirties and have set nothing in motion. I could die tomorrow and it wouldn't leave a scratch. I hate being trapped here. I'd leave today if I could. I'm going to send in résumés for jobs."

"Visiting them last night has upset you."

"I guess it has."

"You're attracted to Pari." She was amazed at her own frankness.

"I *was*." He looked away from her as if ashamed.

"Are you still?"

"I have you now."

Then he left. Minou had an impulse to run after him, to encompass him completely in her embrace so that nothing of him was left for anyone else.

A few days later, shortly after Javad came home from school, there was a knock on the door. Javad went to open it before Minou had the chance to. Then he stood there talking to someone whose voice was unfamiliar to her. Although she could not hear their words, something quarrelsome about their tone disturbed her. Then their footsteps sounded in the corridor. In a moment she heard them carrying on a conversation in the living room. She went into the corridor and listened.

"What kind of political statement are you trying to make?" the visitor was saying. "Do you have any idea yourself?"

"That some fanatic group has set out to murder people for—"

"What makes you so sure there was any group behind it? It seems to have been an accident."

"It's impossible. Someone had locked up the exit doors and then, while people were suffocating inside, no one, none of the ushers even, was in a rush to report the fire."

"I happen to be a member of Bandeh Khoda, the group you've accused of being behind the fire. I have every reason to be upset."

"Do you admit you bought out *Ijtemah* from the newsstands?"

"I already said no. But I'm here for a different purpose." There was a threat in his voice. "I'm here to defend my brother's honor. It's a matter of pride."

"What are you talking about?"

"Don't you know, really? Before, I only had a suspicion, but now—"

"You're trying to blackmail me." Javad sounded breathless.

"If you don't settle—"

"I don't have anything to settle with you."

"Well, then..."

Minou could hear footsteps coming toward the door.

She was about to walk away, but the visitor opened the door and came into the hallway.

He looked startled to see her. "You must be Javad's wife." She nodded.

Javad came out. "This is Karim Soleimani, Rahman's brother," he explained. And to Karim he said, "This is my wife, Minou."

"I'm happy to have the pleasure of meeting you," Karim said.

"The same here," she said stiffly.

Karim was immaculately dressed in a starched white shirt and a pair of dark blue pants. He resembled Rahman, but he was a little shorter and looked older.

He began to walk toward the outer door. He turned around and said to Javad, "Think about what I said."

Javad did not reply.

The door was slammed shut.

Javad looked strained, his manner inhibiting questions. But Minou asked, "What was he saying about defending his brother's honor?"

"He's trying to blackmail me," he burst out. "I used to spend a lot of time with Pari when Rahman was busy at the hospital. Rumors started. That was all two years ago and has nothing to do with now."

"What rumors?" Blood rushed to her face. Her ears were hot.

"That something was going on between Pari and me."

"Was there? Is that why you stopped seeing Pari and Rahman?"

"Rahman asked me to keep Pari company while he was busy working. Then people began to talk."

"Karim seems like a strange man, very different from Rahman," she said, trying to push down jealousy.

"He is. The two brothers are almost exact opposites. Rahman basically wants to be left alone and to leave others be. He's absorbed in his work. He's as much of a nonbeliever as Karim claims to be a believer in traditional values."

"Karim looked sinister."

Javad put his hand on her arm in a tentative way. "Don't worry about him. He just wants to make sure I don't write anything else about Bandeh Khoda. He admitted he belongs to it. They're a reactionary group, trying to destroy progress in this country."

Javad left for his study. Minou could hear him pacing in rasping, clumsy steps in his room. Her blood kept racing.

Minou was walking home at twilight. A little boy came out
of the adjacent alley and approached her. "Lady, this is for
you." He handed her an envelope.

She stared at it—her name was written on it in ink.
When she looked up she saw the boy running back into the
alley. There was no one else on the street, but she hesitated
before opening the envelope. Finally she tore it open and
began to read:

Dear Mrs. Partovi,

I am taking the liberty of warning you about a matter
that has been unsettling to many of us in Abadan. It concerns your husband and a certain shady, I may say more
explicitly, immoral, act he has been engaged in. It's par-

ticularly upsetting since it has to do with Dr. Rahman
Soleimani whom many of us admire and love for his kind-
ness to the poor he treats on his own time. We do not want
his name to be dragged down. For now it suffices for me to
let you know that, without going into detail about it. It is a
matter of conscience on my part to intervene, to give you
the chance to do something about it, perhaps talking your
husband into leaving Abadan before he is harmed by someone who might be even more outraged than I am.

The letter ended abruptly. It was not signed. The handwriting was ornate, each word carefully drawn in black
ink. A blind rage rose in her. She tore the letter into pieces,
threw the pieces into the gutter, and walked away. Obviously Karim had something to do with the letter. Then she
regretted having thrown it away. Now she had nothing to
show Javad.

Once home, she sat on the veranda and stared at the familiar scene to calm herself. Fish floated in the pool. Sparrows flew out of the parapet at the edge of the roof. When
Javad came home she told him about the letter.

"Let me see it," he said.

"I tore it up and threw it away. I was very upset."

"You shouldn't have done that. Was it handwritten?" A
touch of vulnerability flashed across his eyes.

"Yes."

"I might have been able to tell who wrote it from the
handwriting. I'm sure it's Karim's doing, though. He wants
to drive me out of Abadan so that he and his group can
carry out their fanatic ideas without any resistance."

"You ought to speak to Rahman about it."

"I don't feel comfortable with that."

"What does Karim do? He has all this time to meddle in
your affairs."

"He deals in rugs, exports them to Japan, but obviously he still has time to spare."

"I wish we could leave Abadan immediately."

Javad was pursuing his own thoughts. "He had come to school again and talked with the principal about the course in religion he wants to introduce. He had mentioned to Mr. Yabi that I sent out the article on the fire. Mr. Yabi called me into his office. He advised me to stay away from that kind of thing."

"You sent out an article?"

"We reprinted the one we had in *Ijtemah* by itself and sent it out to a list of names. Karim must have gotten hold of a copy."

"You're going to get into serious trouble if you aren't careful. Asghar was imprisoned over what he wrote."

"That was different—it had to do with an article directly critical of the government."

"Still, you're taking a risk."

"This is the last of it. Mr. Yabi warned me that if we persist it would harm the school. We might begin to get complaints from parents who are the supporters of Bandeh Khoda." Javad looked a little shaken. "Next time anyone approaches you in the street, ignore him."

Minou agreed, but her apprehension lingered.

Shopping at the bakery, she encountered Zohreh, the young woman living across the street. Zohreh greeted Minou and then said, "We got the article about the fire. My husband wasn't pleased about the accusation against Bandeh Khoda implied in the article. Not that he belongs to the group, but he believes in what they stand for."

Minou was taken aback. "Javad is entitled to print what he thinks is the truth."

"He's starting trouble," Zohreh said coolly.

Minou paid for the pastry she had bought and left. What right did this woman she barely knew have to talk to her this way? Abadan was even smaller and more claustrophobic than she had thought.

She hardly had time to talk to Javad these days. He either came home late and exhausted and went straight to bed or spent the evening working in hard concentration at his desk. There was a veiled look about him, making her wonder if he was about to write something in *Ijtemah* that he did not want to discuss with her.

"I wish we would talk more," she complained.

"We talk . . . don't we?"

"Not enough. It's so isolated for me here."

"I'm sorry."

"Tell me, do you love me?"

"Of course I do."

"You never say so."

"Is it words that are important? I want to make you happy. I want so much for the two of us to be happy."

But she was aware of an invisible rift between them.

Minou and Ali had gone to the Square. After looking around for a while they sat in the outdoor section of a restaurant to have tea. The checkered white and red oilcloth on the table was sticky with sugar. Flies kept coming to it and Minou waved them off. The tea glasses had a yellowish color. Whirls of dust rose in the air as a bus or a horsecart went by. From where they sat they could see the dome and minarets of a mosque, and the flame of the oil refuse burner, almost blending into the sunlight.

A small boy with a patch over one of his eyes came over to them and begged on and on until Minou gave him some money. Then he ran to another table and held his hand out before the customer sitting there.

"I'll be leaving Abadan soon," Ali said.

"You could stay a little longer if you want. I'm sure my mother wouldn't object. She has Zahra with her."

"It's my fate...." He looked distracted, staring at something in the distance. "Someone is following us."

"Who?"

"Look at the man standing behind that tree. Every time we came out of a shop he was standing somewhere near."

She glanced at the scrawny palm tree on the other side of the Square, where Ali pointed. A man wearing dark glasses was leaning against the tree, his face turned in another direction. "I don't know who he is."

A crowd began to collect in the middle of the Square.

"Something is going on there," Minou said.

"The magician probably. He comes here every week."

"Shall we go and see?" The sight of the strange man in dark glasses had made her uneasy. She signaled to the waiter to come over. She paid, then she and Ali got up and joined the circle of people.

The magician stood in the middle of the circle with a snake wrapped around his neck. He was holding a narrow-necked jar in one hand and a bird in another. Minou could not identify the bird with its striking combination of black, yellow, and red feathers. The magician closed his eyes, whispered something, and then ordered, "Now." The bird began to go in and out of the jar as if it had no bones. "I can decapitate this bird bloodlessly."

Everyone focused on him.

He held the head and the body of the bird in each hand. "Here," he said and pulled his hands apart. The bird was split into two parts with no blood coming out of them. A hum rose from the crowd.

"I don't know how he did that," Ali said.

"The bird must be plastic," Minou said.

"It can't be. I heard it shriek," a woman standing next to her said.

Minou noticed the man Ali had pointed out, standing in the crowd on the other side, glancing at her furtively.

The magician went around and collected money in his hat. Then he picked up his belongings and left. The crowd began to disperse. Minou and Ali started to walk toward the bus stop. Ali was constantly falling behind her, distracted by shop windows. She became aware of a shadow following her, then her name being called. She went into a bookstore and stood between two shelves, looking at books. Some of them were old and stiff with an accumulation of dust.

"Excuse me," someone said. "May I speak to you?"

She turned around. It was the man Ali had pointed out to her.

"We met, remember? I'm Karim Soleimani." He removed his glasses.

"Oh yes." This time he was casually dressed in khaki trousers and a yellow shirt with several of its buttons undone, revealing a gold pendant with "Allah" inscribed on it on his chest.

"I've been wanting to have a talk with you."

"About what?"

"Can we sit somewhere?" His manner was both threatening and confidential.

She thought of the letter. "I'm sorry, I have to go home," she said, looking toward the door for Ali.

"You must get Javad to leave Abadan or else I will have to do something about it."

"You have no right to talk to me like this." She started for the door.

He grasped her arm. "Listen to me. I don't want to involve an innocent girl like you in the mud of Javad's life, his wrongdoings. But how shall I put it, it's my honor, my brother's name is being soiled."

"I have no idea what you're talking about."

She pulled away her arm.

"Don't you really know about her?" He stared into her eyes. "Pari."

"Why are you hounding us?" Her voice was trembling. The store spun around her head.

She walked outside. He caught up with her.

"If you don't get him to leave, I'll..."

She was relieved to see Ali approaching them. "Ali," she called to him.

"I hope you understand the gravity of the situation," Karim said and walked away as Ali was about to reach them.

"I was right, he was following you," Ali said. "I'm sorry I lost you."

"He's just a troublemaker."

"What did he want?"

"Nothing. I didn't pay attention to what he said."

As they turned into a narrow street, they were caught in a crowd, a procession of men walking in long, brisk strides and whipping their shoulders with chains or beating their chests with their hands, chanting, "Allah-o-Akbar," and "Ya Hussain," mourning the suffering of the imams in this month of Muharram. Two of the men walked ahead of the others, holding a banner with the name of Imam Hussain embroidered in green against a black background. Four men walked behind them, banging cymbals to the rhythm of the chant. Some of the men had shaved their hair, some had long, henna-colored beards. They all wore black trousers and black shoes and shirts, stained with blood from the wounds they were inflicting on themselves. A mass of people followed them on the sidewalks, others leaned out of windows and rooftops, joining in the chant.

Through the open doors of houses Minou could see prayer sessions going on. Shoes people had taken off were piled in the doorways of rooms.

It was an arduous process for her and Ali to push themselves out of the throng. At one point she thought she saw Karim chanting with the crowd.

The bus came right away and they got into it. A little girl sat in front of them and kept smiling at Minou and talking to her. Did Minou like her barrette, her red dress? That distracted Minou, but as soon as they were out of the bus Karim's voice began to ring in her ears: "My brother's name is being soiled."

Javad was home, sitting in the living room and listening to records. He called to her, "Minou, where have you been?"

She went into the room.

"What's the matter? You look upset." He turned down the phonograph.

"Karim was following me. He said I ought to talk with you about—"

"This is what I hate about Abadan. It's full of people like him. Don't pay any attention to him."

"He said something about Pari again. He said you'll be sorry if you don't leave Abadan."

"He's trying to blackmail me. I told you that."

"Have you seen Pari since that night?"

"No," he said flatly. "You've worked yourself into a state."

A clear image of the visit came to her, the way he had been totally rapt in Pari and how she had felt herself fading.

He went on, "Don't you see how false this all sounds? Why isn't he letting Rahman into this, why isn't he punishing Pari? He knows that I know this is simply blackmail."

Minou plopped herself on the sofa and stared at the two plates Farzin had given her, hanging on the wall—the festive scenes depicted on them of women dancing. A few days previously she had received a letter from Farzin that she was leaving for Tehran to stay with her aunt and to attend the university the following year. That had given Minou a pang of envy.

Javad sat next to her and gently pushed his fingers through her hair. He said, "I know it has been hard for you. It will be different for both of us when I have a new job in a bigger place. Then there will be more opportunities for you. I've been sending out résumés. Something might turn up."

"I hope we can leave soon."

At the beginning of winter the heat abated. It rained on and off almost every day. Finally Ali was leaving. Minou and Javad took him to the wharf. They loaded his luggage into the boat and waited. He had collected a great many things since he came to Abadan. He held his parakeet cage in his hand. The parakeet was excited and kept repeating, "Salaam."

The water was the color of bronze, streaked with purple and black. The tide was low and the bank strewn with thousands of crabs, minnows, empty snail shells. Fishermen bent over the water, their fishing poles forming parallel lines. Ships were going by. Minou recalled standing by the Kārūn River in Ahvāz and dreaming of going away. How quickly those dreams had awakened again.

She imagined herself on one of those ships, sailing far away.

The boat hooted and passengers began to embark. Ali shook hands with Javad and then held Minou's hand in his, swinging it back and forth. "I'm leaving," he said. "But if it's God's will and I'm alive, we'll see each other again."

"Here is a present for you. I almost forgot to give it to you." She handed him a cigarette lighter with a picture of the Eiffel Tower that he had once admired in the Square.

"May God protect you." He took the present and rubbed it between his fingers, beaming. Then he went to the boat.

As soon as they turned around to leave, it began to rain in huge, rapid drops. Children, excited by it, jumped up and down and opened their mouths, licking the drops. Javad and Minou ran toward the bus and taxi stands. A bus was waiting there and a crowd rushed to it, fighting to get on. Another bus pulled in and Minou and Javad got into that one. Water dripped from their hair and arms.

By the time they got home the rain had stopped and a thin moon stood in the sky. Javad changed and left for a meeting he had about *Ijtemah*. At the door he said, "I'm not sure what time we'll be finished. Don't wait up for me."

Minou sat on the bed in her robe and looked through a magazine. Her mind kept wandering. She picked up the notebook and pen she kept on the table and tried to write a story, something she had been attempting for a while, but nothing would come. Nothing ever came. The dryness inside her upset her. She was like a stream that had gone too long without a rainfall. Where was this day-after-day leading to? Wake, eat, walk, sleep, in different orders but all the same. It occurred to her that she was waiting again, as she had all her life, for something to resolve itself. Marriage had not changed that. A sad picture of her mother sweating and complaining came to her. She had renounced the life of her mother and aunts, but it was not clear how she was to take up a different life.

She looked at the large calendar hanging on the wall. There were four months left to the end of Javad's school term. She had to bear this period and then she hoped they would be able to leave for a bigger city where she could do more with herself. But what would happen if no jobs came Javad's way? They certainly did not have enough savings to live on for a long period of time. They would have to stay.

A cool breeze blew in through the windows. She wrapped herself in the quilt that had been a present from Narghes. A toad hopped onto the windowsill and ran back into the courtyard. Bats darted back and forth under the canopy on the other side of the courtyard. Ali used to find bats on the ground and complain that they were bad omens and should be gotten rid of. Soon his room would be occupied by Fatollah, the man who had worked for Javad previously.

The phone began to ring. She reached over and picked up the receiver. She could only hear shallow breathing. Then someone said, "Do you know where your husband is right now?" The voice was unfamiliar.

"Who is this?"

There was a pause. Then, "Do you know where he is?"

"What are you talking about?"

"He's with her, Pari."

Minou hung up. Her hand was trembling. It had been a strange voice, not clearly that of a man or of a woman. It could have been Karim disguising his voice or someone else taking orders from him.

An hour later the phone rang again. She let it ring. The ringing stopped for a moment and then started again. This time she gave in and answered it. As she had suspected, it was the same voice, giving her the same message. "Do you know where your husband is?" She slammed down the receiver.

She lay down and closed her eyes, hoping to go to sleep.

Then she heard Javad turning the key in the door. "I'm so glad you're back," she said as soon as he came into the room.

"What's the matter?"

"I've been miserable. I kept wondering where you were."

"Where I was? At a meeting."

She told him about the phone calls.

"I'm sure it was instigated by Karim. Who else?" Javad said.

"He said you were with Pari tonight."

"That's absurd." He added in a mocking, hurt voice, "You want me to provide you with an alibi?"

"Have you seen Pari since that night?"

"You asked me that before, I said no."

"You're so late."

"We had a lot to discuss. There's clearly a new conservative sweep in Abadan. The Zenith Cinema being burned down was only a beginning." Javad began to undress, looking preoccupied. He had not kissed her as he usually did when he came in. He put on a robe and said, "I have to work a little at my desk."

Minou turned out the light, but she had a hard time sleeping. She kept thinking of Pari, her haughty face, of Javad's admission to an attraction between them in the past. What was she to make of it all?

The next morning they had their breakfast on the veranda as usual. The courtyard was fervid with the noise and roaming about of animals—frogs, a variety of insects, birds around the flower beds, goldfish in the pond. She could not really take pleasure in them—the anxiety of the night before was still with her.

Javad looked up from *Abadan News* and said, "You're just a child, a wonderful child." He patted her head. Then he stroked her arm, her breasts through her blouse. The switch from one to the other, protection to lust, sent a thrill of excitement through her. She rubbed her head against his arm. He pulled her to him and kissed her.

The two of them lay in the hammock, tightly entwined, swaying a little, listening to the breeze thrashing through the leaves. He was very quiet, subdued. For the moment it was enough just to lie there with him, in peace.

But as soon as he left, the agitation began to throb in her again.

She looked through the newspaper for job advertisements. She recalled the brief encounter she had with a movie studio and her satisfaction at earning money on her own. But here in Abadan, with an abundance of trained people, foreign or Iranian, who would know exactly what companies to go to? There seemed to be no opportunities for her.

Through the long afternoon she wrote letters. Thinking of her friends made her nostalgic for her school. She could almost hear the murmur of the conversation in the washroom, everyone confiding in one another.

She wrote to Farzin: "My marriage has turned out to be different from what I had expected. I hope it won't dissolve into the kind we dreaded, remember? It has not made me whole. It has only divided me. Again I've begun to dream of going away. I envy your freedom, going to school next year. I stand by the river and watch the ships...."

She wrote to Sohrab: "If I had stayed unmarried long enough, maybe Father would have let me go away like you. Sometimes I feel if I were given a ticket and permission to leave I would join you immediately." She imagined herself there, in that country into which she had only glanced. She hungered for wide cool parks, tall glittering buildings, snow falling and falling, sitting in classrooms and offices side by side with men. But it was none of these specific things. It was that other, more intangible thing, imbedded in idealized pictures on the screen.

Whatever negative things Sohrab had written to her about the United States did not register. That he was beginning to see there was something sterile about the uniformity, that he had a hard time forming more than casual relationships with the girls he met, that he yearned for sudden and impulsive ferment between people, that he missed the Persian language, that he still felt foreign.

None of this had much meaning for Minou.

She mailed the letters with anticipation as if she were buying lottery tickets, hoping for something to happen.

16

On a late afternoon Minou visited a historic mosque, now converted into a Moslem seminary school. It stood in the Arabic section of Abadan like an oasis with its golden dome, stained-glass windows, and a lush green courtyard.

She went inside through the archway and walked along with other visitors. The air was soft. Pigeons peeked out of spaces in the parapets. Ancient trees, crouching a little, lined the cobblestoned paths. White-robed students sat on a balcony, talking or poring over the Korans on their laps.

A sign informed visitors that they were welcome to go into the students' living area. She climbed the stairway and entered a room furnished starkly with a rug, a few pots and pans, and shelves holding books. A student lay on the cot, seemingly oblivious of his surroundings. She went through the row of other similar rooms and then came back down and sat on a bench. In a moment she became aware of someone standing before her. She looked up. It was Pari.

Pari had been so much on her mind that her presence there, in flesh and blood, seemed unreal. Minou could not take her eyes off her. She kept starting to assess her reality.

Pari was staring at Minou, too. Then a playful expression came over Pari's face as if she were delighted to see Minou.

"Do you come here often?" she asked.

"No, this is the first time."

"I noticed you up there in the rooms, but I wasn't sure if it was you until you sat here." She sat down beside Minou. There was a faint smell of jasmine perfume about her.

Minou had been conscious of someone always being behind her as she walked in the seminarians' residential area and, turning to go back down, she had seen the straps of sandals and the edge of a wheat-colored skirt. It had not occurred to her that it would be Pari.

"Rahman and I hoped we would hear from you again. What happened?"

"I guess . . . mostly Javad has been very busy." Pari's presence, though arousing pain, enlivened her. She was the only interesting woman Minou had met in Abadan.

A tall blond man came and sat on the bench across from theirs. He began to read a magazine in English. He was holding a portable radio, turned on low. A woman's voice singing in English filled the air, sounding incongruous in the ornate, dusty garden. Pari kept glancing at the man and others passing by. She touched her ankle—a tiny leaf had stuck to it. She seemed nervous.

"Abadan is a dreadful place to live in, isn't it? You must be finding that out by now," she said, focusing on Minou again. "Everyone is cooped in with heat and dust, the horrible smell of the petroleum, dirty water. And so little to do. Night after night with one or two movies around to see, no decent restaurants. It's stagnant, you can't get out of what you step into."

Minou could see that Pari wanted her to like her, a contrast to her seeming indifference the first time they met.

"I know exactly what you mean."

"Rahman and I don't understand what has gotten into Javad. We still look back wistfully on those days when the three of us were students and the early days in Abadan. We spent every moment we could together. We were full of hope, optimistic. He must have talked to you about us."

Minou tried to overcome her timidity with Pari. "He said there was some tension among the three of you."

"Did he really say that? We thought he might have blown up our little disagreements." Pari looked dismayed. "He isn't an easy person to understand. After all these years Rahman and I still don't feel we really know him."

"I'm beginning to think I don't understand Javad myself. Maybe I had invented him to begin with." It amazed her that she was speaking so openly with Pari, but she had not talked intimately with anyone for a long time.

Pari encouraged it. "Javad is very different from the way he used to be. All three of us have changed. We're saddened people in some ways. Outwardly Rahman is a successful man. He likes his work, he's dedicated to it, but often he's depressed by the hopeless state of things he sees every day in his profession. And Javad, the newspaper he works so hard on, I wonder how much satisfaction it gives him. He has very little freedom to say what he wants." Pari looked down at the ground, keeping her eyes there for a long time. Then she said, "All those limitations are multiplied for a woman."

"I'm finding that out, more and more."

"Here in Abadan we're exposed to the values of the West but aren't allowed the freedom the Westerners have. It's like someone dangling a golden chain before us and pulling it up and up so that we can't reach it. It's too late for us to get out of the rut, but you're young, maybe you can still do something about your life. I said that to Javad."

"You just saw Javad?" It was as though a cold hand were squeezing her heart.

"No, not recently. It was some time ago, the night you both came over."

Something about Pari's tone, a hesitancy, made Minou mistrust what she had said. Another Pari seemed hidden beneath the visible one, showing a little and hiding again. The current between Pari and Javad was there even in his absence. It was in the way Pari pronounced his name, the familiarity, the exuberance tinged with pain. Pari evoked in Minou the feelings she once had about a young woman she encountered when she was on vacation with her parents. The woman was going up a hill, accompanied by two young men. She leaned on each man intermittently or held their hands as she came across difficult spots. She smiled at one and then the other. Her hair was short but it blew over her forehead with a breeze. There was an air of great freedom about her that had stayed with Minou.

"Someone like Karim might be better off in some ways. He's stayed with the tradition, believes in the *chador*, in arranged marriages," Pari said.

"I met Karim. He came over after Javad wrote about the fire."

"I'm not surprised."

"He said he's a member of the group Javad had accused of having a part in starting the fire."

"I knew he would be at least a sympathizer. Rahman

and he rarely see each other these days. The coolness between them was inevitable, they're so different."

Minou wished she could bring everything into the open,
tell Pari what Karim had said about her and Javad, ask her
question after question until she was satisfied with the
meaning of all that was happening.

She looked into Pari's eyes, the black eyes in whose
depths Javad's heart was perhaps trapped, entangled as if
in seaweed. But the eyes revealed nothing at the moment.

Pari went on, "I must admit Rahman and I are very
hurt by Javad's coolness toward us. I guess we should have
talked things out more."

"That isn't an easy thing to do."

"It's interesting to Rahman and me that Javad married
someone as young and, well, innocent as you."

Minou blushed, conscious of an inadequacy.

"He was always resistant to marriage. He said it would
restrict him. We speculated what his wife would be like if
he ever did marry."

Minou stammered, "What kind of a woman did you
imagine?"

"We didn't have a clear-cut picture. We thought
perhaps he . . . no, we couldn't begin to guess, but you're a
good choice for him, I can see, perfect in many ways."

The compliment seemed to mask something—disap-
proval, jealousy?

Minou was becoming uncomfortable under Pari's
scrutiny. Pari's judgment of her, she realized, was of para-
mount importance.

Pari went on, "In fact, now that I've met you I can't
imagine him with anyone else."

"You're very kind."

They both looked away. People were coming and going.
The blond man had left the bench.

The jingling of donkey bells going by outside filled the garden with a sudden, unspecific sorrow. A gleam of sunlight lingered at the top of the highest palm fronds.

Minou looked at her watch. It was six o'clock. "I'd better go, it's getting late."

"I'm expecting someone at six-thirty here, in connection with my work, otherwise I'd walk back with you. I hope you'll visit me at my house—will you?"

"I'll try."

"You and I could be very good friends. I don't see why we shouldn't be, on our own. We don't have to interact as couples necessarily. I see I can talk to you."

"Thank you. I thought you'd know a lot of people."

"Not anyone I like that much. I'm often on my own. I don't warm up to people easily."

"I'm flattered."

They said good-bye and Minou walked away. She went back through different streets. The houses were ramshackle, the trees parched and withered. The sidewalks were stained with blood from slaughtered sheep or chickens and with urine. In a narrow lane a woman was leaning over the gutter of water, washing her hair. A group of Arab women wearing long robes walked by in tandem, holding pots carefully balanced on their heads. Minou was very thirsty, almost dehydrated. She stopped by a stall and bought a glass of carrot juice and drank it in a few gulps.

In the hallway of their house she could see Javad sitting at his desk with his shirt off, working. The thought of his being in love with Pari the way she had hoped he would be with herself, with a palpitating desire to possess her, made her almost physically ill. She went over to him. He lifted his head, looking a little startled. "I didn't see you coming in. Where did you go? You're flushed."

"I walked all the way to Kuwaiti Mosque and back." She

added quickly, trying to sound lighthearted, "Guess who I saw. Pari!"

"Pari? Really?" He looked incredulous. "Purely accidentally?"

"Yes."

She could feel, almost touch, his displeasure.

"Well, it's a small place. Sooner or later you run into people you know," he said.

She wanted to press him to talk about Pari, his feelings toward her, but when she tried to utter the questions they seemed absurd, at the level of hints and hunches, nothing concrete. Pari was right. He was a difficult person to really understand.

She stared at his naked back. She craved for warmth from him. She put her arms around him and kissed his neck, his shoulders. He took her into his arms and kissed her on the lips. But she thought there was something hollow about his kiss.

She walked away thinking, I will have to stop focusing on him so much, I must find other channels for myself.

Since Ali had left, Minou spent several hours every day doing housework, but a sense of aimlessness persisted. She thought of the possibility of having a child, of all the talk with her aunts about the importance of fertility and how a woman's life isn't whole without children, but she could not gather a real desire for one. At the beginning of her marriage, her absorption in Javad had prevented it. Now there was a reverse reason, her vague awareness of a rift between them. Again she tried to focus her attention on writing something, but the dryness was still there.

Finally she began to be excited about an idea—she could try to start a magazine. She might be able to get the women she knew to contribute to it, stories, poems, essays, printing just a limited number of copies in an inexpensive format at first. She could not handle the whole thing alone, but she would try to find someone to collaborate with her. She thought of all the people she knew. Pari came to her mind. She, with her interest in art, could help a great deal, doing the illustrations and designing the layout. It would be her redemption if she managed to put it into practice, what she needed to lift her days. Then she began to vacillate. At times it seemed overwhelming and impractical.

In less than a month, Fatollah, Javad's previous servant, arrived, holding a suitcase in his hand and a bundle under his arm. He was tall and muscular, but his movements were slack like an athlete past his prime. He knew the house well and began to make himself comfortable again in the room he had lived in before. He hung a dark brown cloth over the door to keep out the light. He dragged himself into the room as if he were entering a cave. He said he liked the peacefulness of having that room to himself, away from his family. His wife and three children lived in Khorramshahr, and he would spend his days off with them.

He talked incessantly. "I want to be independent one day. My wife has been pressing me to open up my own shop, to sell fruit or groceries. She says our children are growing up and she wants them to be proud of me. Why should anyone be poor here when oil springs up like water from the ground? It's a disgrace for anyone to be poor in this land."

But he complained about the refinery. Since it was built many plants had been destroyed or stunted because of oil leaking into the river. When he was a child Abadan and all the surrounding towns were lush with flowers and trees bearing fruit. There were many more kinds of fish. All the houses had high sturdy walls around them, none of these flimsy bungalows. Now the blackness that contaminated the water also seeped into the souls of people, making them dissatisfied.

He knew all the local vendors. A farmer brought his cow to the door and milked it into a bucket in front of Fatollah. Then Fatollah boiled the milk. He also bought lamb that way. A shepherd slaughtered one every week in the little alley nearby and sold pieces of it to a regular number of families.

He told her about the neighbors.

"There were several English and American families living here, on this street. They all left. They couldn't bear being separated from their own people. Just as well, they were taking over. You know that young, plump woman living three houses down?"

"I've seen her."

"She's married to a rug merchant. Her mother-in-law was visiting last year and there was constant fighting among the three of them. He once beat her because she insulted his mother. You should have heard her cry. But who knows, maybe she was really disrespectful of his mother." Fatollah's face grew thoughtful. "It doesn't hurt to discipline your wife once in a while to keep her on the right track. It's up to a man to show he can do that, otherwise the woman will lose respect for him." He rambled on. "That middle-aged man next door, with the sallow skin, he was married to a young woman. She left for her mother's house and never returned. People say he's addicted to heroin and that was why she left him." He added in a whisper, as if saying it quietly made it legitimate for him to tell her, "Heroin takes away your manhood."

She thought of asking him if he knew Pari and Rahman, but he volunteered.

"It's a good thing that Javad *khan* brought you back with him. He was lonely last year. He spent much of his time with Dr. Soleimani and his wife."

"Did they come here often?"

"At least once a week. Dr. Soleimani is a nice man. He always had a kind word for me, has helped out many poor, sick people. But his wife... Sometimes I could hear her laughter all the way from my room. She tried to imitate American women. I'm glad she doesn't come here anymore. There was something"—he searched for words—"disturbing about her."

Fatollah and a woman, Farogh, who worked as a nurse for a family living nearby, often sat on the front steps and gossiped. The woman had come from a village and always wore colorful skirts and a kerchief on her head. She had been hired to supplement breastfeeding the twins born to the family. She looked too old for that—her face was all lined—but her breasts were full, bulging out under her shirt. Once Minou overheard them talking.

"Javad *khan* is a very cold-looking man," Farogh said.

"He keeps to himself."

Then they began to whisper and she only heard Dr. Rahman Soleimani's name mentioned by Fatollah—perhaps he was praising him or making a comparison between him and Javad.

On a quiet morning Minou took the bus to Bream. She would talk to Pari about the magazine. Why not? Pari had invited her friendship.

In daylight she could see how luxurious this section of Abadan was. The houses were large and modern. There was an extraordinary range of green in the foliage—lime, jade, emerald, mixed with the purple of lotus flowers and hyacinths. A white church stood in the middle of the street. Children ran around in the playground not far from the church.

Suddenly a herd of skeletal-looking sheep came into the street followed by a shepherd, holding a stick. The sheep moved slowly, laboriously, and the shepherd kept nudging them, using his stick and making a sound to prod them on. The sheep were clumsy, dragging their dirty bodies. Their wool was matted and patched, exposing raw skin underneath. One of them was missing an eye. Their presence was strange in this neighborhood. They had a smell about them, of hay and dirt, that lingered in the air after they left.

Minou paused by Pari's house. Through a window she could see the coffee table and the corner of the sofa on which she had sat that night. No one seemed to be in the room. A half-open latticed iron gate gave onto a well-kept yard.

How would Pari react to her coming there without notice? Finally she rang the bell.

She heard footsteps inside. Pari herself opened the door. She was wearing a bright pink dress with butterfly designs. Her hair was disheveled, her face free of makeup. She looked prettier that way, Minou thought.

"What a surprise! You came. I didn't think you would."

"I wanted to talk to you."

"Come in." She moved to the side to let Minou in.

They went into a room. The nasal voice of a woman singing flowed in from a radio.

"This is my work space," Pari said, turning off the music. "It has the best lighting during the day and I have those lamps at night." A cluster of large bulbs hung on the ceiling.

Sheets of paper, crayons, paintboxes and brushes, fabrics with various designs were strewn on the floor and on a large table.

"These are the latest things I've done," Pari said, picking up scraps of fabric and holding them out to Minou.

Minou took them, one by one, and looked at them—paisley designs, flowers, butterflies, in different combinations and colors.

"You're lucky you have something like this."

"I don't know what I would do without it." She took back the scraps of fabric and threw them on the table. "Soon I'm going to stop designing fabrics and paint instead. I'd prefer not to be restricted, but this was a start and gave me the satisfaction of making money, dealing in business." She pointed toward a chair. "Do sit down."

Minou sat on the chair and Pari sat on another across from her.

"That's partly what I came to talk to you about, the possibility of your helping me to start a magazine, doing the illustrations for it and maybe the layout."

"What kind of a magazine? First let me get you some tea, then we'll talk about it."

Pari went out and came back. "Sekineh is going to bring it in." She sat down, looking at Minou intently. "What kind of a magazine do you have in mind?"

"A literary magazine oriented toward women. I thought I'd ask women I know to contribute to it and maybe write to some published women writers as well."

"It's an excellent idea. We women need one another to protect us from men." She laughed. "They treat us as if we were different creatures, with feelings and thoughts incomprehensible to them."

"It's true." Pari's enthusiasm immediately lifted Minou's mood.

"Our husbands aren't as bad as some men, but still their sense of loyalty to one another is so automatic. For a long time I felt shut out from their friendship. I kept trying to break into it until I succeeded a little. They began to include me more, listen to me seriously. I trained them to look at me differently."

"So I'm benefiting from that!"

There was a knock on the door.

"Come in," Pari said.

The door opened and a woman, holding a tray, came in. She was middle-aged and wore a plain knee-length dress in brown cotton and a kerchief on her head.

"Sekineh has been with us for several years. I couldn't manage without her."

"May God keep you alive," Sekineh said.

Pari pulled a table between the two chairs and Sekineh set the tray on it. "That's fine. We'll serve ourselves."

Sekineh left the room, shutting the door behind her.

Pari poured the tea from the ceramic pot into the tall, gleaming glasses in silver holders. Then she held the rock sugars before Minou. Minou took a piece of the sugar and put it in her tea, stirring it with a spoon.

"Women in other countries have so many options," Pari said.

"I always wished I could go to Europe or the United States, where my brother is studying. Then I got married," Minou said.

"You made a choice."

"Not quite." Minou smiled. "I wasn't really given the choice."

She wondered, wistfully, if she had really put up enough of a fight. The envy of those women, as she imagined them, pricked her again.

"Why should the husband always get the custody of children?" Pari said. "Why should boys inherit twice as much of their parents' money as girls? I won't have children under these conditions. It gives me a sinking feeling every time I think how little claim I'd have on them if things didn't work out between Rahman and me."

"I can't think of having children now either."

"I didn't even want to get married."

Pari was so cool and self-possessed. It was difficult for Minou to imagine Pari carried away by love as she herself had been. In the grip of self-disgust, Minou said, "What else is there for women other than latching on to a man? In other countries it must be different. Maybe love is more mature. Maybe one chooses better."

"I'm sure at least there's more joy in it."

They both sipped their tea for a moment. Then Minou put down her cup.

"So you're willing to do the illustrations? I won't be able to pay much."

"I'd do it for my own satisfaction. First let us see if you get anything worthwhile to print."

"I'm so glad I came here and talked with you," Minou said, getting up.

"Won't you stay for lunch?"

"Thank you, but I'd better get back." She was eager to start work on the magazine as soon as possible.

At the door Pari said, "Let me know what progress you make."

"Of course." Minou was elated all the way home. She

could not believe it had all gone so well between herself and Pari. There had been such an easy rapport and so much encouragement. Pari had said she would do the illustrations without charge. If the magazine made money Minou would of course insist on paying her. She would also pay the writers. Her mind was soaring ahead. For the time being she had to talk to Javad about the cost of this particular issue, how many copies she should print, how much it would cost. She was sure Javad would be understanding. He was aware of her restlessness.

The magazine was beginning to take shape quickly. She
had written to some of her friends in Ahvāz and talked
with the wives of *Ijtemah* editors and asked for contributions. She had also written to Manijeh Baghshi and
Soorena Davoodi, two women writers who published in
Rahbar, a magazine devoted to stories and poems.

She received something almost daily. Most of the pieces
were crude expressions of everyday frustrations: a wife
bewildered by responsibilities at home; a woman hating
her mother-in-law, who controlled her husband's actions.
But there were a few good, fresh stories and poems. (She
never received anything from Baghshi and Davoodi
—maybe her letters were never forwarded to them.)

She particularly liked a story by Simin, who obliquely
spoke about her experience when Asghar was in jail:

. . . A gloomy drowsiness fell over the house. Something was wrong with it, full of cracks that might widen. It was oppressive with its stone walls, the dark hallway. The living room I liked so much seemed dingy. Everything in it was worn, pointing to a past that had slipped away. A knock on the door made me jump. "Maybe it's him."

When the mailman came I watched the street. I could see children and young men coming and going, but no Bahman riding his bicycle, his shirt blown out. I kept looking every day, thinking of all the other times I had waited for him and he had finally returned. But there was no sign of him, not yet. . . .

Another story she liked was by Soroor, her friend from high school in Ahvāz.

. . . She married a young man who wore suits and a folded white handkerchief in his front pocket. He was educated and worked in an office. He had a ruddy face, thick lips, and tiny eyes and winked at Maryam before leaving for his work.

Maryam began to notice things missing around the house and sometimes she could not find the money she had put on the mantel or in her purse. And one afternoon, peeping into the room where her husband was visiting with a young boy, she found them in an embrace, naked.

She would also include a poem by Forugh Farrokhzad, a poet who had lived in Ahvāz and then moved to Tehran, where she was killed in a car accident. The rumors were that she was murdered by some people who considered her poems to be immoral. In her poetry she openly expressed her passion for men. Once, in Ahvāz, Minou had had a glimpse of her as she passed in a car, and had been struck by the bitter expression on her face.

She read through Forugh Farrokhzad's collected poems several times and finally decided on one that represented her poetry in general:

> *One can cry out*
> *with a voice quite false, quite remote*
> *"I love..."*
> *one can in a man's dominating arms*
> *be a beautiful, healthy female*
> *with a body like a leather tablecloth*
> *with two big hard breasts*
> *one can in bed with a drunk, a madman, a tramp*
> *rape the innocence of love.*

She put aside all the pieces she wanted to include in the first issue and sent them to Pari to look at and perhaps to illustrate. She was a little concerned about those whose contributions she could not print in the first issue. She had not anticipated so many pieces coming in. She would have to explain with letters or phone calls.

Javad had, by and large, stayed out of her way. When she first told him about the magazine he had looked at her incredulously as if what she said had not registered.

Then he said, "You went to see Pari about a magazine? Why is this the first time I'm hearing about it? I don't think it was right for you to go and see her without even consulting me about it."

"I wasn't sure it would be practical, but Pari was enthusiastic. She said she would do the illustrations."

Later he was willing to discuss the expenses. They agreed it would be best for Minou to use the same typist and printer Javad did for *Ijtemah*.

After that, Javad avoided talking to her about the magazine. He was not encouraging or discouraging, just reticent, monosyllabic in response to her questions.

Minou was too involved in the magazine to read all of the next issue of *Ijtemah*. But she read an article Javad had on the front page, in which he argued it was a waste to introduce religion into the school curriculum—that was something students could easily seek out at home instead of taking time from other subjects at school. The article disturbed her a little. It was as though Javad was directly opposing Karim, had him on his mind when he wrote the article. She sympathized with Javad and was afraid for him at the same time.

She hoped to live in Abadan peacefully until they could leave.

Minou called the magazine *For Women*. Though the paper and the printing were inexpensive, altogether the magazine had an attractive look. Pari liked what Minou had selected for the first issue and had done a few small sketches for some of the stories and poems. For the cover she had drawn a fashionable woman, wearing a hat and a short dress, standing next to a red convertible car with her hands outstretched.

On the day Minou got the finished issues from the printers she took a taxi over to the Square with a stack of them, taking a detour first to drop off one in Pari's mailbox. She stopped at the largest magazine stand on the Square.

The owner was a stocky, surly-looking man. "Can I help you?"

"I . . . we have this magazine, it's new, oriented toward women. We wondered if we could leave a few with you."

He looked at her, up and down, so quizzically that it felt like an attack.

"It's mostly stories."

He took an issue from her and glanced through it. "I'm sorry, I wouldn't want my wife and daughter to read this.

We're trying to get rid of this kind of influence, not add to it."

"It's nothing radical, contains nothing—"

"Try another place." He looked away from her, withdrawing so completely that she did not dare to persist.

Minou walked away, her heart sinking a little. She went to another, slightly smaller, newsstand. The man here, a little older than the other, was outright rude. He looked at the sketch on the cover and said, "The dress is too short. Is that the model you want to set for women?"

She was speechless. She had not anticipated such an objection. Her face was hot, flushed. "That's just a picture," she stammered.

Many of the other magazines on his rack had pictures of actors and actresses on the cover, some in similar clothes.

He scrutinized Minou's dress, which came below her knees. "I'd rather see women with veils over their heads."

Minou was treated the same way again and again. "Woman, keep to your own business," one of the men said after she had explained the magazine's orientation. "Go home and attend to your husband and children." She walked through the Square with the feeling of being pushed and carried along with the crowd of people, diminished with each rejection. It was as though they were dismissing her rather than the magazine. The experience reawakened in her the sense of defeat she and Javad had felt when the *Ijtemah* issues were thrown into the doorway of their house. Only this time she had to bear it alone.

Minou had somewhat better luck at the Sun and Moon Bookstore. The owner, a middle-aged, gray-haired man, wearing glasses, was more sympathetic.

"Has this been approved?"

"Does it need to be?"

"If we're caught with something that the government doesn't like we can be put out of business at once."

"This kind of thing has been printed before."

"Recently they've been tightening their grip on us. No one knows exactly what's behind it."

Still he took a few issues and piled them near the register. The large, musty store was cluttered with stacks of old magazines and books, some of which seemed to have been there for years without ever having been touched, collecting dust, torn and yellowed at the edges.

Minou walked to the bus stop with the magazines weighing heavily under her arm. Vendors stood near the bus stop, selling Pepsi, *dugh*, poppy seed pods from which opium had already been extracted. Children were buying some and eating the dried poppies from a little opening at the top. Laborers sat in a row against the wall, eating bread and grapes and winking and whistling at young girls passing by. Women hurried home, carrying loaves of bread, pastry, and fruit. Suddenly a fight started between two men. They grappled with each other while a group of people gathered around them.

"You were looking at her, she's my fiancée," one of the men said hoarsely.

"You ought to tell her to cover herself better. I was looking at her *disapprovingly*, half of her hair was exposed."

That only made the other man more furious. "She was covered up perfectly well," he shouted, his cheeks flushed, his eyes fiery.

The two of them went at each other fiercely, hitting, pushing and pulling. They were sweating and panting heavily.

A young woman, wearing a blue *chador* held tightly around her face, was standing not far from the crowd, crying softly.

A moustached man went forward, jumped between the two men, who had separated for an instant, and said, "Let me settle the fight for you. Each apologize to the other and stop, or else you're going to kill each other."

"It's the heat, it makes people irritable," another man standing by said.

Then the bus came and Minou got on it.

Minou went to see Pari the next afternoon.

"It was very discouraging," Minou said. "Most of them weren't willing to carry them. They thought it wasn't proper. They even insulted me. Only the Sun and Moon Bookstore took some."

"I'm not surprised. But are you willing to fight the hard battle?"

"Maybe we should try a new angle with the next issue, not make it exclusively for women."

"I like the idea of its being only for women."

They discussed the possibility of sending out what they had to a number of people and waiting to see what responses they would get. Perhaps they could build up a readership through subscription. But Pari seemed a little distracted, in a hurry, making Minou wonder if she was blaming her for the failure or if she was losing interest in the project. There was something offhand, almost dismissive about her manner.

"Would you like tea, anything to drink?" Pari asked casually.

"No thanks. I came only for a few moments. For days I've let everything else go at home, I've been constantly working on this magazine."

There was an awkward pause. Then Minou said, guiltily, "It was naïve of me not to have predicted this kind of obstacle. I'm sorry about all the time you spent."

Pari shrugged. "It might still work out. We may get better results through our mailing."

Minou looked at the scraps of fabric on the table. She said, "You must have unfinished work you'd like to get back to."

"No, no," Pari said in a tentative voice.

"I ought to leave anyway."

Pari did not say anything. The lack of words lay like a dark chasm between them.

Minou rose and picked up her pocketbook. She said good-bye and walked out.

She decided to go and see Javad at his school. She had to talk to him. His reticence about the magazine depressed her more than ever.

Minou got off the bus on the wide, busy Shah Reza Avenue, the closest stop to his school. There was a commotion by the Rex Cinema, young boys shoving one another to get to the ticket booth for the next show, an American Western. Actors in cowboy hats, holding horses' reins, were displayed on billboards. Loud, raucous music from the sound track of the movie filled the air. On the other side of the street workers were repairing the Zenith Cinema. They had put a fence around it, closing the area to traffic and pedestrians.

Javad was not in his office. He could not be too far—a book was open on his desk and his glasses lay on it. She thought of the night she had gone to see him in her high school. She had slipped out of her house as if under his spell. That was less than a year ago.

After a few moments she left his office and started looking for him in the corridor. Students had collected there and talked heatedly as she and her friends used to in similar corridors. Some of them started to run and laugh in a giddy way. The bell rang and they all went into the classrooms, taking their seats.

Then Javad came into the courtyard from the hall on the

other side, holding a batch of students' papers in his hands. She called to him. He did not hear her. He went into a classroom and shut the door. She wandered to that side and looked into the room from a window. The small panes of glass were held together by black-painted wood, looking oppressive. The whole courtyard, with its sagging volleyball net, the unhealthy palms and sunflower plants huddling together in one corner, cobwebs weighted down by dust on the moldings, felt like jail.

A girl stood up and began to read. Javad sat behind his desk, resting his chin on his hand, listening. Minou could see his profile clearly, lit by a ray of sun. He was transfigured to that image she recalled from when she had first met him. How blindly she had loved him, how false her hopes of salvation through him had been.

She left the window and started for his office again. In the corridor she saw Mr. Yabi, the principal, whom she had once met.

He bumped into her and said, "I'm sorry. Oh, Mrs. Partovi, welcome to our school. I assume you're waiting for Mr. Partovi." He was dressed in a suit and a tie.

"Yes," she said tensely.

"The session will be over soon." He walked away. A couple of times he turned around and glanced at her as if he found her coming there to be strange.

Minou went into Javad's office and waited. The bell rang. In a few moments Javad came in and was startled to find her there.

"I came to talk to you about the magazine. I wanted to talk to you last night, but you came home so late."

"Couldn't you have waited until this afternoon?"

"Do you know how hard it is for me here? I have no friends and you shut me out so much of the time."

"What about the magazine do you want to discuss?"

157

"The whole thing is so frustrating. Only one place was willing to carry it."

"That's what you might have expected."

"No one has respect for a woman's work."

"You think it's bad for you simply because you're a woman, but don't you see how limited it is for me here? Hasn't that become obvious to you?" He sounded a little more patient.

"It's several degrees worse for me."

"A little more or less doesn't make much of a difference. I don't know what's going to happen to this issue of *Ijtemah*. Karim might collect them from the newsstands again."

"I'm reaching the point where I want to scream," Minou said. "I wish I could leave the country, at least for a while."

"We could never afford that," Javad said. "We depend on my income. Besides, with all its problems, this is our home. Contempt for our own country isn't going to do anyone any good. You're just upset. I've been through worse things and still I keep at it."

Suddenly he reached forward and, for a speechless moment, they embraced. Minou was struck by the emptiness of the embrace and, as they separated, by the look in his eyes. They seemed to be focused on something far away that excluded her.

The bell rang again. "I'd better leave," she said.

"I'll be back home early. I'll make a point of it today."

When she got home the phone was ringing.

"What were you doing visiting the whore? He was with her. . . ."

She slammed down the receiver. She was chilled to think someone was keeping track of her movements. A few days ago she thought she had seen Karim standing in the hallway of the house two doors down from theirs. For an instant she was aware of nothing else but his eyes before he disappeared into the hall.

And was Javad seeing Pari? Was that why Pari had acted so cool today, why Javad had been so reticent?

She felt oddly detached from Javad's belongings—his jacket and tie hanging over the arm of the chair, his desk covered with books and sheets of paper he had scribbled on.

She could hardly bear staying on there. What did hold her down, she asked herself, now that she and Javad were drifting apart, now that she was finding out that Abadan was no better than Ahvāz for her? Perhaps no place in Iran would offer her what she craved for. Sohrab had recently sent her a photograph of himself with a group of men and women standing together in what seemed to be the backyard of a house. They were all casually dressed, their hair windblown. One of the women was barefoot, standing on her toes, her lips turned to a man. He was bent down a little to kiss her. It was a simple thing the photograph had captured, but it had an almost violent effect on her. What struck her was the carefree expressions on their faces that went beyond their smiles, conveying movement, implicit action, freedom. How oppressed she, Javad, and everyone else she knew in Abadan were by contrast. Javad was right—he was not much better off than she was. He could not help her any more than she could help him. The world she had built up around him was slowly disintegrating. He, she, and the others were all in a vast jail together. She must get out. But was she ready to leave Javad? Besides, she would need Javad's financial support as well as his permission even to obtain a passport.

Minou woke in the middle of the night from an anxious dream that she could not recall. She lay there in the dark beside Javad, far away from him, and tried to calculate how much it would cost her to go to the United States. She would need about 7,000 *tomans* for the plane fare and an equal amount to get settled, good for a month or two. The quickest way to obtain a visa, she knew, would be through a connection with a university: even a course in English would be sufficient. There was a public library in Bream, serving mostly the Americans and the English living in the district. Maybe in the morning she would go there and try to find information about schools and possible jobs.

But in the morning, as she went about her routine household chores, the thoughts seemed a part of her dreams.

It was Norooz, a holiday to celebrate the new year, the beginning of the spring. The streets were alive with festivity. Platters of wheat and lentil plants, cultivated for the occasion, were set on windowsills. Children, dressed in colorful clothes and shiny shoes, went back and forth from house to house, visiting, exchanging presents with relatives. In late afternoon they collected twigs and dried branches of trees and made little piles of them in front of their houses. When it grew dark they lit the wood and made fires. They jumped over them, singing, "My yellowness to you, your redness to us," so that they would be healthy all year, their sickness going into the fire.

Some adults let go of their inhibitions and joined the children. Shopkeepers hung pressure lamps on their doors. Even carts had lamps or candles hung on them. Sounds of tambourines, drums, flutes, and violins poured out of houses or shop radios. Men dressed as clowns performed on the street.

As children, Minou and Sohrab had dressed up and visited every relative, jumped again and again over a fire that hypnotized them. They had been allowed to stay out on the dazzlingly bright streets late into the night. They and other children on the block had run through the streets holding lit torches, laughing and singing wildly. But now something dark and troubling seemed to Minou to lie under the glitter.

The day before the holidays began she had gone to the Sun and Moon Bookstore. The few copies of the magazines she had left still sat there.

"I sold one copy," the owner told her.

"You can throw the rest out and keep the money for that one."

"I'm sorry."

In contrast to the initial response from the contributors, few people had bothered writing back about the finished magazine. The spark that they had shown at first seemed to have been quickly extinguished by other concerns. Javad had remained reticent, preoccupied.

Still Minou made some lame motions to celebrate the holiday. She soaked lentils and wheat in water on platters so they would sprout and she put the platters on the windowsills of each room. She and Javad bought each other presents. He gave her a handmade silver bracelet with black engravings of birds on it. She gave him an English kit of comb, brush, cologne, and soap.

One afternoon she, Javad, and the *Ijtemah* editors and their families all went to a park, crowded with people picnicking. Trees were full of buds. Young girls were knotting the long stems of the grass so that their wishes would come true. It was on another picnic that Javad had proposed.

They sat under the canopy of a grapevine. Each family had brought food, some prepared already and some to be cooked there on a fire. Minou had brought rice with ground meat and spices and a spinach pie. As on the first time they met as a group, the men and women were basically segregated. The women asked Minou a few perfunctory questions about the magazine. Even Simin, whose story carried such power, seemed preoccupied by her full-time role as mother and wife. After a while Minou wandered off by herself and did not come back until they were about to go home.

Javad gave an obligatory dinner party to which he invited everyone from his school. Shopping for food, Minou noticed the flies buzzing around dates and raisins, the blemishes on an apple or a tomato, the persistent haggling of customers and sellers, children hovering around their mothers, falling down, screeching, begging to be taken home. There was inertia, passivity, in the mothers' faces. A rush of pity and then helplessness came over Minou. She was going to end up as one of them. Javad was too guarded and remote for her to complain to. His face had a tired, almost resentful look all the time.

Javad and Minou were invited to a few teas and luncheons, given mostly by the teachers, and to a dinner at Mr. Yabi's house, where a lavish meal was served supervised by his pretty young wife (she wore a translucent, light green *chador*, letting some of her curly brown hair and part of her made-up face show). Mr. Yabi bragged that she had made everything herself, including the bread.

Minou's mother called and said, "We haven't seen you since you got married. What has become of you?"

Minou said, "I'll come and visit one of these days, soon."

"Is anything the matter with you?"

"No."

"Are you sure nothing is wrong?"

"Yes." She still did not want to admit to problems, to her disillusionments.

Javad's mother called, also complaining that she had not seen them.

"We should spend some time there this summer," Javad said to Minou. "My mother is too old to travel."

Minou agreed offhandedly, unsure of her future with Javad.

Then Minou's mother and father came over for one night. When they called to tell her they were going to visit, she went around frantically and made sure everything was immaculate and in place. She put several tulip pots in the room they would be sleeping in and her best sheets, in pale blue, on the bed. Only moments before they rang the bell, Minou took a last glance at the living room, rearranged the plants, fluffed up the cushions on the sofa. She looked intently at herself in the mirror to make sure her hair and her light makeup were in order.

Her father seemed stiff and he kept brushing off the dust that had settled over his hair and dark suit on the drive over. Her mother, too, was not at ease and complimented her profusely on the furniture. They were both dressed up, the way she remembered them at the wedding. They seemed a little strange.

They sat on the veranda and ate the dinner Fatollah had prepared (she had made sure he cooked the pomegranate chicken both her parents liked), and drank tea, and Javad and her father drank arak in addition. Her father asked for his tea to be made lighter, for a lemon to squeeze over his chicken.

"I can see you've turned into a good homemaker," her father said to her, smiling at Javad. "Or is this a show for us?"

"No, no, Minou has been good."

There was an awkward silence.

Then her father said to Javad, "This is a very comfortable place. Your school seems quiet generous with you."

"Yes, in some ways."

"In other ways you're unhappy with it?"

"They maintain very tight control of the teachers."

"That's true about being employed by any organization. I went into law to avoid being a civil servant."

"You did the right thing. If I manage to become a university teacher, maybe I'll have a bit more freedom."

"Do you intend to do that?"

"I'm hoping for it."

Minou's father turned toward her. "Aren't you going to talk to us?"

"I had a bad few weeks." The words burst out of her. "I worked hard putting together a magazine, but no one was willing to stock it. Other than housework, there's nothing else I can do here."

"You're going on dreaming. When are you ever going to be content?" her father said.

Javad shifted in his seat, looking uneasy.

"You ought to get busy and have children," her mother said.

After dinner her father and Javad played backgammon, and Minou and her mother sat in a corner talking perfunctorily.

They all retired to bed early. In the morning, after breakfast, her parents began to get ready to leave.

"If there were time I'd go shopping in the Kuwaiti Bazaar," her mother said.

"Why don't you stay longer?" Javad asked. "You ought to consider this your home."

"Thank you, but we must be back. We have so many things to attend to," her mother said rather primly.

"You ought to come and spend the rest of the holiday with us," her father said.

"It's very kind of you, but I've been swamped by work," Javad replied. "I haven't been able to go home and see my mother all year."

"I understand how important work is, particularly at your age."

"She hasn't visited here?" Minou's mother asked, a little suspiciously.

"She doesn't like to travel. She gets sick on boats, cars, and airplanes."

"Some people are sensitive that way."

Then they gave Minou and Javad and also Fatollah money as presents. Minou and Javad gave them the presents they had bought for them, for her aunts, cousins, and Ali—silk scarves and ties, earrings—to take back.

"You shouldn't have done this, you're young, just starting," her mother said.

"They're nothing," Javad said.

They picked up their small overnight bags and left.

Minou walked outside with them. The house seemed a little desolate when she came back inside.

Not long after the holidays, returning home from some errands, Minou found a letter from Farzin on the hammock, put there for her by Fatollah. She was eager to read the letter. To her surprise, Farzin had been among a few of her friends who had not responded to her circular about *For Women*.

"... I've been trying to call you but have been unable to reach you. My uncle and I will be in Bandar 'Abbās on Tuesday for the day. We're traveling around. I will wait for you at Behesht Café on Main Street at eleven o'clock. If you're not there by twelve I'll assume you can't meet me. I hope you can. . . ."

The date Farzin gave was the next day. The thought of seeing her friend was like a fresh breeze. Minou had so much to tell her that she had not said in her letters. Had Farzin changed? In the morning Minou left right after Javad went off to school, to catch the boat to Bandar 'Abbās. She had to get on the first one leaving that morning in order to make it on time. Javad had said, "This should be very nice for you, seeing your old friend."

Minou arrived at the wharf half an hour early. People were standing around talking, their luggage on the ground.

"It's getting crazier and crazier in Abadan," a young woman said to another woman next to her. She was leaning against a large bundle wrapped in a cloth with pretty designs of willowy girls standing behind windows and men with long white beards drinking wine under trees. "People aren't as good as they used to be."

A wind began to stir, bringing a burning smell in their direction.

"The smell is from the American hospital. They burn dead bodies."

"That's because they aren't Moslems. They have no souls."

The time of departure approached and passed. The captain came out and announced, "We're having a bit of trouble; be patient."

There was a hum of protest among the people waiting.

A baby held in a woman's lap began to cry in a fussy, whimpering way that quickly escalated into a howl. She squirmed and waved her hands in the air as if grasping for something.

Minou walked away to the street running parallel to the

wharf. At the corner of the street stood an ancient hollow tree, its branches reaching far out into the air. A hermit lived in the hollow and children hovered around, trying to lure him out.

"Come out, talk to us, do you want some food, coconuts or dates?"

The old man sat in the dim enclosure, staring far away as if unaware of the commotion around him.

In another spot a group of children had formed a circle around a wounded donkey half-sunk in the mud. Some of the children were trying to pull the donkey out, but it resisted and moaned, blood trickling from its wound. Two policemen came over and ordered the children to stop. The children obeyed immediately. The policemen took hold of the donkey's legs and began to drag it toward a Jeep. Blood sank into the sand, making little balls.

Minou went back to the wharf. The captain came out again. "Sorry, patient passengers, the ship won't be sailing for another two hours, in case there are things you want to attend to."

Minou could not possibly be on time for Farzin now. She lingered a few moments and then walked away. The intensity of her disappointment reminded her once again of her isolation in Abadan.

Reaching home, she noticed that the shutters on the bedroom and the living room windows were closed. It was Fatollah's day off. Javad must have decided to come home during his lunch break, something he had not done for a long time. Why would he choose a day when he thought she would be away? She opened the door angrily, thinking of that.

In the hallway she was aware of a familiar scent. Then she heard a conversation going on in the bedroom. A sudden chill went up her spine as she recognized Pari's voice, and at the same time she identified the scent in the air to be the jasmine perfume she had worn the few times Minou had met her.

"There are no alternatives," Pari said.

"You caused me so much pain."

So this is the whole truth at last. I have to believe it now, Minou thought. I can't go on denying it. Her pain was like an animal with tiny furry legs, kicking at every spot of her body.

"What else is there to do?" Pari said.

Minou could hear the beating of her own heart so loudly that she was afraid the sound would carry over into that room, penetrate through the shut doors, but she continued to stand there, paralyzed. The hallway seemed like a vast place with herself a small figure in it.

"I can't, I just can't."

"You will be able to as soon as you decide."

Both voices became inaudible. Finally Minou tiptoed into the courtyard. She sat on the bench on the far side. I must leave him now, at any cost, she thought. I have no choice now, no hope. I hate him. Fish tumbled in the pool. Sounds of laughter and music came out of the adjacent house. The world was not all that bleak, but her veins were hot as if on fire, her mouth had a bitter taste, her breathing was heavy as if she had been running for a long time. She kept looking toward the bedroom.

After what seemed a long time, she saw Pari going into the hallway. She was not sure if Pari saw her or if it was a play of light that made her think Pari had put her hand on her mouth to stifle a cry. Pari walked out quickly, almost running. She was wearing the pink dress she had worn once before. Her image burned into Minou's eyes.

Minou continued to sit in her spot for a while. Then she went into the bedroom. Javad sat in a chair with a glass of water in his hand. His hair was ruffled and he had misbuttoned his shirt. The bed was unmade, the sheets in disarray. Pari's perfume lingered in the air.

Javad's face became a little distorted when he saw her. Then a dark, private sorrow registered on it.

"Did you just get in?" he asked.

"No." Her voice sounded flat to her own ears. A ray of light escaping through the shutters shone on the empty, rumpled bed, where Javad and Pari must have lain.

She sat at the edge of a chair. Neither of them said anything for a period.

Then he looked to the window and said, absurdly, "It's very light out."

"I know Pari was here. I heard her talking to you."

Javad gave the impression of a man about to collapse, who could not be trusted to speak his mind. He merely said, "I see."

After an uncomfortable pause he said, "She came here to see you."

"I don't believe that. This must have been all planned. You thought I was going to be out all day and asked her to come over. You must have been seeing her all along."

"Only twice. Once she came to school to see me and another time I went to her house." He stared at his hands like a guilty child. "It was the old obsession again, taking control of me."

The pain of having been betrayed—by both of them—churned in her. "You're still in love with her."

The word "love" dangled between them.

He reached out his hand as if wanting to touch Minou and then dropped it. "You can be in love with someone and hate them at the same time." He looked into her face directly.

Javad had changed under her eyes from one person to

another. It was like the dream she had a few nights ago. In the dream she stood in the middle of the room with Javad. She kept touching his arm without his responding. Then she realized he was someone else, the man who owned the dairy shop at the top of the street. Her heart was beating rapidly as it had in her dream when she became aware of her mistake.

"I was stupidly and blindly in love with you," she said.

"Love! Love! You've been listening to too many sentimental songs."

"What about you, this love and hate you have for Pari?"

"I'm trapped by it. It isn't something I'd seek out. At one time I thought of her as a way to freedom. She was a substitute for all the risks I didn't take. I could say to myself: I'm doing something that is totally the expression of my own desire. The guilt seemed, at first, a very small price."

Then, to Minou's surprise, he hid his face in his hands and began to cry. "I'm a despicable person. I wish I were dead."

Minou looked at him, in shock. She tried to measure his pain against her own. There was a hierarchy of suffering with Javad, Pari, and herself all locked in it.

Did Rahman know about what was going on? Karim knew. Had he kept it from his brother? What did all this matter to her now? She would leave Javad no matter what the consequences.

He stopped crying and took off his glasses, which had become wet, and wiped them with a piece of tissue. He did that mechanically, without looking at her. He put his glasses back on and got up.

Minou continued to sit, stiff, brooding over the nightmarish turn her marriage had taken, the hollowness of it. She had an awful, helpless feeling.

Javad was pacing the room. He stopped and said, in a preoccupied way, "I had no right to do this to you."

"I've been living *alone*. You were a figment of my imagination." She managed to add, "I'm going to leave Abadan as soon as possible. I want to get out of this country."

"How are you going to do that?" he asked gently.

"I know I have no legal right to my *mehrieh* if I leave you. But you could lend me some money. I'll pay you back."

"Of course, if that's really what you want." He added sadly, "A wife needs a letter of permission from her husband to leave the country. I would have to write one for you."

"I've been thinking about it since the magazine failed, since you and I stopped talking to each other." A momentary sense of relief came over her in the midst of her anguish as she verbalized those thoughts.

"Don't leave me alone here." His voice was almost pleading. "I know it has been difficult for you, but I will never see Pari again. If you like I'll send in a letter of resignation to school to make sure I won't be staying on here, no matter what. I know we can be happy together somewhere else. It will be different once we leave Abadan. We'll go right after school ends. I'll take on any job that comes along and look for something better later."

It moved her that he seemed so much at her mercy. The hard stone of hatred in her chest was melting and she realized, with a vague dread, that unless she was careful she might weaken and stay on with him.

"You and I can't help each other," she said. "Pari isn't the only thing. You know that."

In a few moments he was sitting across from her again. Suddenly it was easy to talk, as if the shock had destroyed the barrier between them.

Pari, he told her, had fluctuated between Rahman and Javad at the beginning when they were students in Tehran, showing more interest in one and then the other, but finally she had drifted toward Rahman. Javad had noticed her even before the three of them became friends. She was one of the few outspoken women in classes, always asking questions, disagreeing with the professors. He recalled exactly how it happened, that first time he kissed Pari. They were still at the university. By then she was engaged to Rahman. The three of them were at the house of one of the other students for a party. Rahman was arguing with someone, about a person's responsibility to his country. Pari walked away impatiently—the argument had been going on for too long. In a moment she called Javad from the kitchen. "This is too heavy on my neck," she said, pointing to the gold necklace, a string of leaves. Javad stood behind her and while she held her hair up he unclasped the necklace. She turned around and put her head on his chest, rubbing her face into it. He took her into his arms and kissed her lightly on the lips and then let go quickly. "We mustn't do this."

"You're right," she said in a matter-of-fact tone that shocked him. How under control she seemed to be!

When they came back into the living room Pari blended back into the party while he sat in a corner stiff and quiet. It had been Pari whom he had held in his arms, he thought, not so much with desire but with astonishment. In a short while he said good-bye and left. But he thought of this encounter later during the long evenings the three of them spent together, sitting in one of their living rooms, depending on whose parents were out, drinking arak, listening to music, and gossiping. Javad had said to himself over and over that it must never happen again and it did not for a long time, not until their work brought them all to Abadan.

Then one afternoon when he was alone at home, Pari came over. Rahman was at the hospital. Again it was she who took the initiative. She got up from her chair and knelt beside him, holding his knees in her hands. Her face looked luminous, as if it were lit from the inside. He leaned over and kissed her. Then he pulled her up and they went into the bedroom. After that it was hard for him to stop himself from seeing her privately. For hours they lay together in bed, sometimes just holding each other. The guilt and pain seemed to render their love an intolerable intensity, dark and bottomless. There was a bitterness to their physical desire, a longing which did not recede in those intense joinings that seemed to happen mysteriously like the swarming of bees. After a while it was no longer desire that held them together but a kind of dark, anxious dependency, their bodies becoming a part of that need to possess the other as thoroughly as possible, with pleasure playing little part in it. The original exhilarating liberation they found in one another's company quickly deteriorated through the very same force that had brought them together.

He tried to break away several times, but all it took was a little encouragement from her for him to start again. She kept saying to him, "I'm happy when I'm with you here, but when I leave, everything changes. I live in constant expectation, as if my whole life were a heartbeat." She looked to him for some kind of nourishment. For him their love, at least at the beginning, was an arena of freedom, an escape from the heat, the injustices he felt he could do nothing about: the smell of oil everywhere, the blackouts, the poverty in spite of the oil. But, he admitted, this could be a rationalization. Perhaps at the bottom he was merely bored with his life, maybe he was envious of Rahman. It was hard to understand his own motives.

When Javad was alone with Rahman he had to restrain himself from confessing, telling him everything and begging for forgiveness. He was not sure if Rahman suspected what was going on. It was the concealment on Javad's part that made continuing the friendship unbearable for him.

Rahman had also begun to withdraw, to become inaccessible emotionally, not only to Pari but to Javad as well. Maybe he had noticed the attraction between them, maybe he was trying to cope with his own disillusionment with his profession—few of his patients recovered, many of them were victims of long hours of work under the unrelenting hot sun, of illnesses gone on too long. He had always struggled, as Javad had, to bring about some change in the condition of things around him.

Javad's meetings with Pari occurred infrequently, once every few weeks, but went on for a year. They softened the edge of guilt for themselves by saying to one another, "This is a dream and we're going to wake up from it one day."

Finally self-loathing took over all Javad's other emotions. His soul became dusty and shriveled like a dry leaf. Pari was also suffering. Excitement had left her body. At one point she said she would leave Rahman so that she could be with Javad without remorse. But she vacillated.

Anywhere else, in a more stimulating city perhaps, Javad would have been able to forget Pari, but here in Abadan she became an obsession. He thought of suicide. Each day was grayer and more monotonous than the one before. His life had become a mockery of what he had expected it to be. He became ineffectual in his work at school and on the newspaper. He knew then he had to get out of Abadan. Now he was back again in the same poisonous environment.

"But I had nothing to do with Pari at the beginning of this year. Karim's accusations were false." He looked a little relieved at remembering that. "I know it sounds strange, but I was drawn to her again partly as a reaction to Karim. It was almost like wanting to prove to myself that I wasn't controlled by him. Now I've told you everything."

Outside, the air was darkening. A flock of birds flew by, Minou could see through the window, tinted by the rose of the sunset. The voice of the muezzin began to fill the air.

Javad said, "I was lonely until you came to my office that night in Ahvāz. I really thought you could save me."

But she kept visualizing him in Pari's arms, responding feverishly to her touch.

20

As the minutes passed, slowly, Minou knew with absolute certainty that everything between her and Javad was finished. In an attempt to purge himself he had made Minou into an object, someone who would hear him out and even console him. He had spared nothing talking about Pari.

She kept thinking about Pari, stung by her betrayal. How could Pari have kept her recent meetings with Javad a secret from her while they were having all those conversations about men? Was it merely empty talk when Pari had said, "We women need each other"?

That night she waited until Javad was asleep before she went to bed. The insects were carrying on and on. She lay there restlessly for a long time before she finally fell asleep.

In the morning, as soon as she was finished with

breakfast, she began to write a letter to Sohrab. Javad had left for work.

"...I'm leaving Javad. So much went wrong. At this point all I want to do is to come to the United States. Javad is willing to give me a loan and permission to leave. Later I'll have to think of a way of supporting myself...."

She went on to ask him to send her the necessary forms for colleges at their parents' address. She mailed the letter and began to pack. She would take the boat to Ahvāz the next morning. She packed the most important things, the necessities. She ached with a desire to be on her own, free to come and go. Her parents would be surprised to see her. Still, it was better just to go rather than to call. She had so much explaining to do. Her heart sank at the thought of that.

When Javad came home in the afternoon he had a present for her, an immense bouquet of tea roses.

Minou averted her face, trying not to show any reaction. She was not in fact sure of her reaction.

He put the flowers, which were already in a pretty green vase, on the table.

"Let's go out tonight," he said. "We could use that. How about the restaurant at the Luxor Hotel? It's supposed to have a nice atmosphere and good food and entertainment."

"I'm not in the mood."

"Please, let's go." He looked at the suitcase she had packed. "You aren't serious about leaving, are you?"

"I must leave."

"Let's go out tonight anyway. What's the use of sitting here and brooding?"

She gave in out of exhaustion of the spirit. What difference did it make if she spent the evening in or out with him?

The restaurant was almost filled when they arrived. Most of the guests were foreign, speaking in different languages, English particularly. Although the hotel was modern, the decor was Iranian. The walls were covered with tapestries of mountains and streams, of lovers embracing under trees. Ornate brass lanterns hung from the ceiling. Blue tiles covered the floor.

The waiter brought over the food, the same for everyone—caviar, kebab, rice, wine to drink. A woman in a glittering silver dress and heavy makeup came onto the platform and began to dance.

Minou thought, Tomorrow I am taking the boat home, but how uneasy that word "home" makes me, no real comfort in it, no consolation. My father is going to say, "You chose him, you'd better stay with him." My mother: "Do you know the disgrace this will bring us if you don't go back to him?" My aunts: "Your head is full of unrealistic ideas."

Then, the next moment, there was that leaping-ahead force inside of her, as if she were propelled by something far off in the future. She would join Sohrab, start fresh, a new life in that distant place into which he had vanished.

The singer looked at the ceiling or the floor, rarely at the audience. Her voice dropped low at times, became like the whimper of a child. The last line, before she suddenly stopped singing, sounded like a shriek. She left, and a comedian came on, telling jokes alternately in Persian and English. Finally there was dance music. Couples began to dance to the slow waltz.

Minou and Javad left. They had hardly talked. Javad seemed as tired and dispirited as she was.

The sound of music followed them, dwindling in the night air.

Javad suggested they walk part of the way back. Brilliant moonlight flooded the streets. The palm leaves clicked in the wind. A camel was snorting somewhere.

As they entered a narrow lane, a voice said, "Hey, you,

stop, stop." A man caught up with them and grabbed Javad's arm. Javad struggled to break loose, but the man put a gun to the side of his face. "Don't move or I'll shoot." He sounded cold, blunt.

"What do you want?" Javad asked.

A yellow Volkswagen pulled up in front of them.

"Get into the car," the man said.

Javad made a confused, resisting motion with his hand.

"Get in," the driver of the car, a rough-looking man, ordered Javad, waving a gun at him.

"Where are you taking him?" Minou asked, cold with fear.

The men ignored her.

Javad went to the car. The first man held the door open and Javad got in. The man sat beside him.

"Javad, I'm afraid," Minou said.

Javad, coming to himself somewhat, said, "Don't worry, go home and wait."

The car pulled away, quickly gathering speed. Minou could see the outline of Javad's face through the back window for a moment before the car turned into another street.

She stood there, in a daze, not knowing what to do. She wanted to go home immediately and call the police, but no buses or cabs were going by.

A solitary figure came into the alley. First she had a fleeting glimpse of his face, a half-formed image as if she were recalling someone from memory. Then she saw him clearly. It was Karim, like a figure in a nightmare.

"Come, let me take you home," he said without explanation.

"What are they going to do to him?" Her voice was hoarse.

"They will take him to the desert and beat him up, then they'll take him back to your house."

"What right do you have—"

"I have every right. This is nothing—I could do much worse things to him." He pointed to the pendant inscribed with the word "Allah" he was wearing again. "If He had wanted me to be Javad's executioner that would have come to me. His will is behind everything."

Suddenly the charred face of the corpse she had seen being carried out of the Zenith Cinema appeared to her, making her shiver.

"I'm going to call the police," she said.

"That won't do you any good."

She began to walk away rapidly. The street was bordered by mud walls on one side and shops on the other. The shops were shuttered. Lean, elusive cats scavenged through the garbage on sidewalks.

Karim caught up with her and began to walk alongside her. He looked composed, formal. His walk was purposeful, as if he had planned every step precisely. She decided to let him walk with her. In a superstitious way, she thought perhaps her good behavior would somehow affect Javad's fate in the desert. Karim's threat, her fear, had brought out in her a sense of protectiveness toward Javad.

"That newspaper Javad publishes is full of lies, designed to stir people up, to convert them to. . godlessness, corruption," Karim said. "If I had wanted to, I could have him arrested for writing that false propaganda, but I only want to save him. I'm not his enemy. In fact there was a time when I liked him."

"He tries to write what he thinks is the truth."

"He has brainwashed you. Don't you see that he writes for self-aggrandizement, it has nothing to do with the truth. I admire courage and conviction in a man. We have a history of martyrs in our religion, men who would give up their lives for their beliefs, but it's different with Javad. His rebellion doesn't have a clear shape as far as I can see."

"He's against oppression of any kind," she said.

A car zoomed into the street, almost hitting them. Karim grasped Minou's arm and pulled her with him onto the sidewalk. A wave of sexual excitement went through her. Then, quickly, it turned into revulsion. How could she feel that when Karim's men might be harming Javad right then, when he could have had a part in the killing of those people in the fire?

Suddenly he laughed. "Oppression! A fancy but empty word. We need more restrictions, more clear-cut values. The fire in the Zenith Cinema is an indication of how easily we can all be destroyed. We don't need people like Javad to stir things further."

Minou looked at Karim's profile, but she could not see the expression on his face in the dim light.

He went on. "If we don't watch out the whole town will go up in flames. It's so volatile here these days."

"So you admit you were trying to blackmail Javad, to stop him from writing certain things? All that talk about family honor was just nonsense."

"Don't you understand that his relationship with Pari is a part of the corruption he's spreading?" Karim was quite cold now, pronouncing every word incisively, as if to make sure she understood him completely.

They entered a crowded street with men and women sitting on the front steps of their houses, talking, children holding on to the lampposts and going around and around. An Arab woman sat on the sidewalk with crocks of yogurt in front of her for sale. Minou had an impulse to shout for help.

Karim scanned the faces for a moment. Then he said, "Pari was in your house yesterday. I was watching." He brushed back the curls of hair that had fallen over his forehead. His face glowed darkly with malevolence. "I heard rumors about it two years ago, but I couldn't quite believe them. I thought they were spread by people jealous of my brother. But this year I saw for myself."

"Javad regrets . . ." she stammered. "He didn't want any of it, he fell into it."

"That doesn't excuse him, his being a weak person. I'm sure he has talked to you about his father's death when he was just a small boy? That must have had something to do with his being a weak man. He never had a father's guidance."

"That has nothing to do with it." Minou was unexpectedly offended by his analysis of Javad's character.

Karim had another explanation. "Maybe he wants to die young, like his father."

"Is that how you justify your criminal acts against him?"

"I'm merely carrying out my duty."

She said very softly, wondering to herself, "Maybe Pari never loved Rahman. Maybe she's always been in love with Javad."

"Of course she loves Rahman. He's superior to Javad in every respect. She's been carrying on with Javad merely to amuse herself. If you give a woman freedom, she will abuse it." He went on vehemently, "She's the devil incarnate. If she were cut with a knife, she would turn into her true self, an ugly witch, all guile, her hair gray, her skin wrinkled, her eyes red, like those witches who came to our kings in disguise to make them commit sins and lose their throne." He stopped and spat on the ground.

He had described Pari with such disgust and condemnation, with such barren hatred, that Pari's real face vanished before her eyes, replaced by the demon face he had described.

Several taxis came in their direction.

"Let me take you home in that taxi." He went to the

curb and held up his hand. One stopped in front of them and they got in. He gave Minou's address to the driver.

In the taxi he said, "You understand that you must get him out of Abadan—he may have a chance at salvation somewhere else. You're living with a mere void, a person sunk into darkness. What do you get out of that?"

She did not reply.

The taxi stopped at the top of the street and she ran out, away from Karim.

As she approached their house she recalled that Fatollah had taken an extra day off. She would have to face the house alone. Was Javad brought back yet?

The door was locked. She opened it and went in apprehensively. In the hallway she called, "Javad, Javad."

There was no answer. She went from room to room and turned on all the lights. She looked in the courtyard. Javad was not back. She lay on their bed with her clothes on and waited. She comforted herself by thinking of her childhood, her brother sleeping in his room next to hers and her grandmother on the porch, the sound of their breathing, the familiar shadow of the palm before the window. Then she was dreaming. She saw the singer in the restaurant floating in the sky, the silver on her dress blending into the stars, Pari with that witch face Karim had attributed to her, and a horrifying sight that made her heart beat loudly, Javad running and running in place in the desert, shouting for help.

Someone was moaning. She opened her eyes. Had she dreamed it? The moaning started again. It sounded very near. She jumped out of the bed and went outside. Javad lay slumped on the ground before the door, with one hand stretched over the stone step.

She knelt down beside him. The lamplight reflected on his skin like yellow dust. She could see cuts with dried blood around them on his arm, his chest, the side of his face. His eyes were closed, his breathing shallow.

"Javad, get up, you're home."

She began to shake him.

"Get up, get up."

A faint odor of blood reached her. What if he died? She should get him inside and then call a doctor. Rahman was the only doctor she knew. Javad would not like her calling him, she was sure. But what choice did she have?

She tried to lift Javad from the ground. She held his arms and pulled, but she was thrust forward by his weight. Finally she managed to get a firm grip on him. She began to drag him slowly up the two steps and through the hallway into the bedroom.

She put him on the bed and sat on a chair, catching her breath. After a moment she got up and laid his head in a comfortable position on the pillow. He had stayed unconscious through all this. His skin had a chalky pallor. She went to the phone to call Rahman. She hesitated again—she did not want to talk to Pari. Finally she dialed, thinking she would hang up if Pari answered the phone.

"Hello."

It was Rahman's voice.

"Hello, this is Minou Partovi. I . . ."

"Minou Partovi, what a surprise. Is something wrong?"

"I'm sorry to bother you, but I need help. Javad was beaten up by some men. He's unconscious."

"Beaten up?"

"We were walking home and these men came over and took him away at gunpoint."

He did not wait for her to explain further. "I'll be right over."

She heard the receiver click. She hung up also and waited, sitting on the chair by Javad, watching for a sign of his regaining consciousness, thinking, I'll be leaving Abadan, this country. What's going to happen to him?

Soon he opened his eyes. His eyes strayed past her. "What am I doing here?" He did not seem to know what had happened.

"Oh, I'm so glad you're all right. You were lying unconscious outside and I brought you in."

She heard a car braking in front of the house. "That's Rahman," she said and ran to the door before Javad had time to say anything.

She opened the door hastily. Rahman stood there, holding a leather valise. He looked immaculate, his hair freshly combed, his clothes in order even though he had been called over in the middle of the night. Did he know about the incident? Had he expected this call?

"Where is he?" he asked, coming in.

"He's in bed."

They walked into the bedroom.

He sat on the chair beside the bed. "Javad."

"Rahman, is that you? I heard your voice but I thought I was dreaming. For a while I was dreaming about a pack of dogs following me, and before that I saw myself burning in an oven." He sounded delirious.

"What did they do to you?"

"Did you hear a knock?" Javad asked.

"You're still dreaming." Rahman took out some instruments from his briefcase. He listened to Javad's heart, then took his blood pressure. He did all this so gently that it seemed like a gesture of affection. His movements, Minou noticed, were measured. He possessed the controlled charm of a person who had learned early on never to let go.

How much did he know? Did he know anything?

He examined the bruises. "From what I can see the wounds are superficial—still, I must take you to the hospital. I may need to give you some tests."

Javad shook his head. "No, no, please. I want to stay here."

"You were unconscious for at least half an hour," Minou said.

"I don't want to go to the hospital," he said with finality.

"I can't force you against your will," Rahman said. "Who were those men who did this to you?"

Javad looked at Minou as if to assess how much she had told Rahman.

She gave him a reassuring look.

Javad said, "I don't know. I had never seen them before."

"But they must have had a motive. Did *Ijtemah* have anything to do with it?"

Javad's face was flooded with so much pain that Minou thought he would break down and start talking, but he merely said, "They didn't explain anything."

"You must report it to the police."

"What good would it do me to go to the police?"

"You're going to let them get away with it?"

"There isn't really anything I can do."

Javad searched the room with his eyes as if hoping to find an area untouched by Rahman's presence. Minou could feel his shame and his loneliness. It was only a matter of time until he and Rahman would talk openly. But she hoped they would not begin until she was out of Abadan.

Rahman asked Minou, "Do you have some cotton and alcohol? Also boiled water. I have bandages here."

Minou went to the bathroom and then into the kitchen, getting what she was asked. She came back and, under the sheet, she and Rahman took Javad's clothes off, carefully—in places his clothes were matted to his skin. Rahman lifted the sheet enough to look at the condition of the bruises. "They're all on the surface. A few will have to be bandaged."

Still keeping the sheet on as much as possible, Rahman began to wash the blood off with cotton dipped in the boiled water, now cooled to lukewarm, and then in alcohol. There were blue marks everywhere on Javad's body. In a few spots the skin was scraped off, exposing the flesh. One wound began to bleed, brightly, shockingly. Rahman held a piece of cotton on it for a moment. Then he dried each wound and put a bandage on it. When he was finished with that he took out two yellow capsules from a container and gave them to Javad. "Here, take these."

Minou gave Javad a glass of water standing on the table. He took the pills and lay back, looking fatigued. Soon he fell asleep.

"He should take two of these every four hours. I'll leave the bottle with you. After that you can remove the bandages and let him take a shower. Call if you have any questions, but I think he's going to be all right. The color is already back in his face." Rahman started for the bathroom.

Minou sat on a chair, listening to the water running,

thinking she would have to stay with Javad until he was well. Rahman came back and stood in the middle of the room, looking aimless.

"Would you like something to drink?"

"No, thank you. I have to go back."

He shut his briefcase and picked it up. They walked to the door. In the hall he said, "Javad and I were so close once, but something happened." He held his gaze on her and for a fraction of a moment she thought there was a flash of acknowledgment there.

She wanted to talk to him, to ask him questions, but she was too exhausted and he was in a hurry. Perhaps he still loved Pari deeply and did not want to lose her by confronting her. Perhaps he knew only a little and saw something awful in it—so he avoided putting the pieces together.

When he reached his car, he rested his hand on its door and looked at her. Then, without saying anything, he got into the car and drove away.

Minou slept in the hammock on the porch. She woke, wet with dew, the sun shining into her eyes. She went inside immediately to check on Javad. He was sitting up on the bed, looking toward the window.

"How do you feel?" she asked.

"Aching a little."

"Would you like breakfast in bed?"

"Please."

She went into the kitchen to get breakfast. She came back with the tray and put it on a table between them. They both toyed with the food. His face and arms were covered with bandages.

Javad said, "I had a dream about my father last night. He was standing with me in a stark white room, telling me something about his work at the Ministry of Education.

There was something he wanted me to do and I agreed to it. Then I woke. I kept thinking about his death again. As I lay there in the dark, I was certain that he had not died accidentally, that he was murdered."

"It would be so easy for Karim to arrange . . ." She could not bring herself to say: your death. A sense of disaster still clutched at her heart. "That was a terrible thing—what happened last night."

"I was right that Karim's antagonism toward me has a lot to do with *Ijtemah*. The two men last night accused me of printing false things, blasphemy. They kept saying, 'Do you promise to stop telling lies?'"

"Did you promise?"

"Of course not. That's why I'm in this shape."

"Next time it might be worse."

"You don't really mean for me to withdraw from the paper? I could never live with myself then. No, I won't give Karim the satisfaction."

"I had to stop my magazine."

"It's not the same."

She sighed, exasperated. She wanted to ask him more questions about the men, the beating, but he looked vulnerable, full of shame and wounded pride. A rush of sympathy for him came over her again, engulfing her in his plight. It was with an effort that she separated herself from him. She thought, If I stay on here we'll drown together.

He went on, "It was only later that the men brought up Pari, by way of blackmail. Of course they were instructed by Karim what to say and do. I'm sure all their words and movements were calculated."

"Karim hates Pari, from the way he spoke about her."

He looked at her intently. "He talked to you about her?"

"Last night. He walked with me until a taxi came by."

"He must have filled you with negative talk about me, as

well," he said gloomily. "But what does it matter, you have your own views of me now. It's funny, but last night when we were in the restaurant I saw how unhappy I've made you. I kept thinking I'd make up for it, if you gave me the chance. I thought I'd beg you to give me the chance. I imagined a place for us in Tehran near the university, an apartment with a view of the Elburz Mountains. I felt sure I'd find a job."

An awkward pause followed, lasting for a moment. Neither of them looked at the other's face.

He turned to the window and waved his hand. "It's a little cloudy."

The gesture, the remark, reminded her of coming into the bedroom after Pari had fled from the house. But then he had said, "It's very light out," as if he could not bear the thought that so much of the day was still ahead of him.

Juxtaposed on this Javad was the Javad of her fantasies. She had hoped, foolishly, to stay permanently at that high, magical state that for a period of time had transcended everything ugly around her.

He said, "Won't you change your mind and stay on here with me?"

"There's no point."

Javad stayed home for a few days, resting in bed, reading and listening to music, but he seemed in a turmoil. He kept looking at the clock. Minou suffered with him the slow monotony of time trickling out of the brass hands of the clock. The bandages reminded her of the threat surrounding him.

He called Mr. Yabi and told him he would be absent for a few days. "I was in a terrible car accident. I'll explain later. You'll have to find someone to substitute for me . . . no, please, it's very kind of you, but I'd rather not see anyone while I'm in this shape. . . ."

There was a barrage of phone calls, people asking after his health, pressing to come over and visit him. Javad refused to see anyone, even the *Ijtemah* editors, who were the only people he had told of the beating. If one of the phone calls was from Pari, Minou had no knowledge of it.

Finally Javad was well enough to go back to work. As soon as he left for school, Minou began to pack again. She would leave the next morning.

Someone was in the courtyard, saying something. She looked out of the window. An old woman was sitting in front of the pool, which Fatollah had emptied that morning to clean. Her hands were folded on her lap. A pair of wooden sandals lay by her side. It seemed she had been there for a long time. She was talking to the sparrows hopping around a flower bed.

"You creations of God. You must see so much wrong in this world, flying above houses and streets, looking and saying nothing. But God must love you to have given you wings."

"What do you want?" Minou asked, going into the courtyard.

The woman's clothes were dirty and ragged. The edge of her *chador* was wet and full of holes from her chewing on it. Her skin was dry and there were cracks at the bottom of her heels. She had hundreds of wrinkles on her face.

"Is that you, the wife?"

Fatollah came out of his room. "I've been trying to get her to leave, but she insisted on seeing you. She wants to tell you something."

"Let her tell me. What is it?"

"Dr. Rahman Soleimani saved my daughter's life. She had blood in her stool. She vomited blood. For two years no one could cure her. She was like a skeleton. Then Dr. Soleimani agreed to see her. It was like a miracle."

"He's an excellent doctor," Minou said, trying to sound calm.

"But I want to talk to you about your husband," the woman said.

194

"Is something the matter?"

"You must stop him from his . . . sin. I'm here in the name of the martyred Husain, who came to me in my sleep, and Lady Fatima, whom I begged for the recovery of my daughter. I went to her shrine on my knees and begged her." Her voice trembled. She was about to cry at the memory.

"What are you talking about?" Minou said faintly.

"She doesn't live in this neighborhood. I don't know where she comes from," Fatollah said, holding the woman's arm and lifting her off the ground.

She put her sandals back on, mumbling, "Your husband will be put in chains and dragged through boiling water into the fires of hell, where he will burn over and over for years." She threw her hands up into the air, making the birds sitting at the edge of the flower bed fly away. "There are no birds in hell, no flowers."

"It's hell right here," Fatollah said, "in this hot, ugly town." He put his hand on the woman's back and gently pushed her forward.

The woman started for the door. "Whoremongers," she said.

In a moment Minou could hear the door banging shut and the woman's wooden sandals sounding on the street.

"She forced herself into the courtyard," Fatollah said.

"Abadan is full of this kind of person, intruding into others' lives." Minou went inside and quickly finished packing. She would not wait for Javad to come home. She would go to the wharf and catch the next boat to Ahvāz. There was time for that if she hurried. She had to settle many things with Javad, financial matters, the terms of their separation, but for now all she wanted was to be out of there as soon as possible.

She wrote a brief note to him: "I'm leaving on the boat to Ahvāz this morning. I count on your promise to give me a loan and a letter of permission to leave Iran. Please send them to Ahvāz. I'm sure you understand." She was not sure what else to say. Finally she just signed, Minou.

She put the note on the table under the vase of flowers he had brought to her. The flowers were withered and some of their petals had fallen, making a pink heap on the floor. Then she took off her wedding ring and the ruby ring that belonged to his family and put them on the note.

Outside, she walked rapidly, propelled by the same urgency that had made her leave before Javad came home. She stopped on Eight Metri Street to get a cab. All the taxis going by were carrying passengers. She decided to walk.

A dusty wind had been blowing for the last few days and everything was ashen. People looked restless and irritable and got into open arguments on the street. Some stray cats were fighting shrilly. Then a hum of obscenities and curses masked all the other noises. As Minou walked on she realized what it was. A group of men and women were picking up stones from the ground and throwing them at a woman who was running in her direction. Their faces were angry and ravaged. They seemed an extension of the old woman who had come to her house. Then she recognized the running figure, like a mirage suddenly turning into concrete reality—it was Pari. She was warding off the stones with wild, nervous gestures of her hand, her hair blowing around her, her eyes unfocused. Her heels made a clomping sound.

Minou stood with others watching on the sidewalk. The sight made her dizzy A nauseating confusion of emotions filled her.

Pari came very close. A stone hit her neck and she ducked her head. A trickle of blood was flowing down her arm. Her dress was smeared with dirt. An impersonal loathing—defiance—burned on her face. Her eyes were like those of an animal in danger.

An image flashed across Minou's mind of Pari lying limp on the ground like a bird that had been shot down and collapsed in a heap of bloody feathers. For a fleeting moment it seemed as though she were joined to Pari, feeling some of the blows aimed at her, the cold impact of physical pain and humiliation.

She thought of the venom in Karim's voice that night as he had spoken about Pari. Was this provoked by him? Was the old woman coming to her house taking orders from him? But perhaps rumors were spreading by themselves in this small, claustrophobic town. She looked around to see if Karim was peeking out from anywhere, but she did not see him.

Pari was several yards away from her now, but the jasmine perfume she always wore lingered behind her.

Two bedraggled men came running into the street from the adjacent alley. "We're going to catch up with you," they shouted to Pari.

Pari ran faster.

"Do it with us too, we'll pay you for it," one of the men said. "Whore."

Pari ran into the Chase Manhattan Bank, which stood among other public buildings on the other side of the street. The two men followed her.

Gradually the people began to scatter. Only a few bystanders remained there, speculating about what might have caused the terrible incident.

"Who was she?"

"She must have done something."

"What? Do you know?"

"Shameful things."

"She's Dr. Soleimani's wife. He's such a good doctor. He does wonders."

"That he should be brought down by a woman like her."

"She has no morals."

"They say the two men were friends, the doctor and the teacher."

"A woman can bring men to ruin."

"Men can be weak, easily tempted by a woman."

Minou looked at her watch. The boat would leave in five minutes. She began to walk rapidly toward the wharf. At the curb, in the shade of a tree, a letter writer was sitting with a stool in front of him, taking dictation from an older man. She used to do the same thing for Ali, writing to his family what he dictated in a flowery, elaborate style. The thought of Ali brought a wave of comfort to her.

The white boat was waiting. The river looked like a shiny sheet of gold under the sunlight.

As soon as she took her seat in the cabin a great fatigue came over her. All the horror of recent days clung to her like poisonous dust.

The image of Pari hit by stones lingered. Once, as a child, her way was blocked by a group of boys on the street. One of them pulled up her skirt and looked underneath and the others laughed. Another time she was standing at the edge of a desiccated valley—she was not sure how old she was then or why she was there all alone—and she had seen a woman running over the rocks at the bottom of the valley and a man following after her, shouting at her to stop. The man caught up with the woman, grabbed her arm, and slapped her. Her blouse was torn and her breasts exposed—round, firm breasts, all scratched and bloody. Minou was oddly humiliated, as if the woman's plight were her own. Watching Pari had brought out the same feeling in her, making her momentarily forget her anger at her.

But now she wished she could run back, grasp Pari's arm, and, looking into her eyes, ask, "Why did you do that to me?" She was too stirred up to sit still. She got up and went to the deck. She stood in a shady corner and looked into the river. Then she could see the bridge over the Kārūn River in Ahvāz, all its lights twinkling.

She woke in the morning by the glare of the sun in her eyes.
A yellow butterfly was flitting around the room. Outside,
the vendors called to people to buy their cheese and milk.
She could hear a spatula hitting against a pan, glasses jingling. She could smell cinnamon and fresh bread from the
kitchen.

The evening before, there had been a flurry of questions
over her unexpected visit. She had said she was tired and
withdrawn to her room.

Minou got out of bed, dressed, and pulled the curtains
open. Through the window she could see the dentist across
the street going around his office, doing things with various
instruments, carrying on his routine as before she left. He
might notice her and wonder about her being back home.
The thought oppressed her, reminding her of her uncertain

state. She would wait until her father left before she went to breakfast. He spent the mornings out, doing business. She preferred to speak to her mother first.

There was a knock on the door. "Minou, are you up?" It was her father. He opened the door without waiting for her to reply. She could instantly see alarm on his face.

"It's all here." He waved a newspaper at her. "That's why you came home." He handed her the newspaper.

The headline "Woman Running Away from Punishment" caught her eye immediately. She read the article.

A woman identified as Pari Soleimani was stabbed by two men in the Chase Manhattan Bank in Abadan yesterday at 12:30 P.M. The security guards came to her aid. They put her in a taxi and asked the driver to take her to the Refinery Hospital, but midway she must have changed her route. There is no record of her at that hospital or any other. No one knows her whereabouts. Her husband, the noted doctor Rahman Soleimani, refused to comment. She had taken refuge in the bank from a group of people who had been throwing stones at her on Eight Metri Street. According to several witnesses, the antagonism against her was provoked by the prevalent rumors to the effect that she was committing adultery with her husband's friend, a teacher at Danesh High School. The friend, Javad Partovi, and his wife could not be reached for comment. . . .

Blood rushed to her face.

Her father was still standing in the doorway.

"Now you come to us. What do you expect me to do for you? To force Javad to take you back?"

"I don't want him to take me back," she mumbled. "I'm leaving him."

"What do you mean, leaving him!"

"I'm not going back there."

"People are going to talk, to ask questions. I've been an honest lawyer all my life. I never took a bribe from anyone. I've kept my name clean and honorable and now you're soiling it."

"I will go away. I've always wanted to go to the United States. I wrote to Sohrab and asked him to send me application forms."

"What will a young woman separated from her husband do in a country like that? You will be prey to every man's—" He checked himself. She knew he was going to say, "lust." He went on, "And where are you going to get the money? You have no claim to your *mehrieh* if you leave Javad." He seemed to be making an effort to keep calm, but his voice was shaking a little.

"Javad agreed to give me enough money to get out of here." She said that firmly, but a sudden apprehension came over her that perhaps she was taking it too much for granted. She had mentioned the idea to Javad only once and he had agreed to it then. . . .

"All this was going on without your ever saying a word about it to me. We were there two weeks ago. You could have said something then."

"I wasn't sure what was going on, what I wanted to do."

"You sound absurd! You insisted on marrying Javad and now all of a sudden you want to separate from him."

Her mother came into the room.

"I'm late for work," her father said suddenly and left.

"What happened?" her mother asked. "Your father showed me the article."

"Do I have to talk about it? I'm separating from Javad."

"What do you mean?" her mother asked, startled as her father had been.

"I accepted the bad with the good in my marriage. You'll have to do the same thing." Her mother's unhappiness was palpable. "You insisted on marrying him. It was your own choice. All men run around, what do you expect?"

"It wasn't just that."

"All your dowry is still there. You will have to go there at least once and get those things."

"I'm sure he'll ship them back here eventually. He won't keep what doesn't belong to him."

Her mother shook her head and then left the room also.

Before long her two aunts came over. Minou sat with them and her mother on the porch, a platter of fruit before them. They ate the pieces of fruit that they had peeled, sliced, and arranged on a little platter and talked. Her mother and aunts' talk about men in general started again: their selfishness, their irrationality.

"You can no more stop a man from his urges than a child from peeing," Narghes said.

"A woman has to make all the compromises," Mehri said.

"Javad isn't going to pay for what he did," Narghes remarked. "You and the other woman will."

"They do what they want and we women pay for it," her mother said.

"It's best not to think of happiness on this earth. This is a place we pass through. Real life begins when we die," Narghes said.

Minou's mother and aunts went on for a while, interrogating her about Javad.

Finally Narghes got up. "It's getting late for our prayers."

Her mother and Mehri got up too. They went into the courtyard to pray.

Ali asked Minou to read to him from his old book as she used to. She was not sure if he had any idea what was happening to her. He kept his polite, almost formal distance. Only once he hinted at knowing something.

"Abadan was full of crazy people," he said.

"I'm leaving Iran. I'm going to join Sohrab."

Tears suddenly gathered in his eyes. "It was enough that Sohrab *khan* went away."

She visited her friends. Their lives had remained predictable. Mahroo was going to marry an officer, a colonel in her father's regiment. Soosan had a promising suitor, a wealthy businessman who owned several rug shops.

They were disappointed—no, horrified—that she was back home already, leaving her husband, as they themselves were just anticipating their own marriages.

"You really couldn't take it?" they said.

The conversation between them kept collapsing. It was as if they looked at her through a mist, not quite recognizing her.

Farzin, at the University of Tehran, was her only friend who was doing something with herself.

Once Minou had to pass through the street where Javad's mother and aunt lived. She walked by the house slowly, overwhelmed by the memory of her wedding night there. The gauzy curtains of the room were drawn, and in the shadowy interior she could make out a fragment of the mirror in which she had first seen herself and Javad together, a single reflection.

Every day she looked through the paper for more news about Pari and Javad, but nothing else was said. In a moment of panic that Javad might not carry out his promise of sending her the money and a letter of permission to leave the country, she called him at the house in Abadan. She called several times, but there was never any answer. If she did not hear from him in a week she would have to turn to Sohrab for financial help. He had started to work as a teaching assistant while he still went to school. She did not want to turn to her father.

A voice was always humming inside her, telling her she must leave Iran as soon as possible.

After their first confrontation Minou and her father rarely talked about her separation from Javad. At mealtimes or when they passed in the hallways they were reticent with one another. Several times she saw lights burning in her father's office when she woke in the middle of the night. Once she got out of bed and looked in. He was sipping arak and reading a leather-bound legal book. But from a kind of questioning expression that sometimes registered on his face it seemed to her he did not quite believe she would stay separated from Javad for long, that it was only a matter of time until she would come to her senses.

Her mother also was a little disbelieving.

"You'll get tired of this and go back to him, won't you?" she kept saying.

"No."

Her mother would bring up the question again in a few hours even though Minou's answer was always the same.

For the first time Minou's mother seemed solicitous of her state of mind. If Minou slept late she would come into her room and wake her up, saying, "Did you have a hard time sleeping?" If Minou did not eat something on the dinner table, her mother fretted, "You don't have any appetite." If Minou stayed late in her room for a period of time, her mother called to her, "Come out here, it isn't good for you to be alone." It was as though Minou's separation from Javad was the only unhappiness her mother could truly understand.

Ahvāz began to blend with Abadan, full of dust and flies, the air contaminated with petroleum fumes, filled with a dense, moaning chorus of noises. People passing by had a resigned look on their faces. It seemed as if they were moving slowly through a gigantic web.

As she looked out from the balcony at the vast market across the street with hundreds of carts heaped with fruit, vegetables, smoked fish, and other foods, with women busily shopping and children crying and tugging at them, the sense of mass helplessness that Minou had begun to feel when shopping in Abadan returned to her.

Going through the empty rooms where her grandmother and Sohrab used to sleep she was aware once again of a hollowness in herself, but now the feeling was intensified, had a dark, heavy weight.

By the end of the third week she heard from both Javad and Sohrab. Javad had sent her a check and the permission letter along with another letter. The check was 20,000 *tomans*, larger than she had hoped.

> ...I'm sorry not to have written sooner. I had to leave Abadan. Mr. Yabi advised me to resign because of the

gossip. He was nice about it and said he would write to the principals he knew in other schools around the country and try to find me a job. But I've decided to stay away from teaching for a while. I'll work at any job I can find and try to get a doctorate. However, I'm not going to Tehran directly. I'm traveling around a bit. I hope the check will cover your plane fare and expenses for a couple of months. This is all I can afford. I will send my address to your father once I'm settled somewhere so that we can make more specific arrangements. . . .

The postmark on the envelope was Kermān. It occurred to her that he might be with Pari. But what difference did it make now?

Sohrab had sent her various forms to fill out and encouraged her in his letter to join him as soon as possible.

She went into her father's office when he was alone. She told him about the letters and then sat down across from him stiffly, staring at his wide, cluttered desk, waiting for his response.

A few desultory moments passed as he asked her questions about the letters.

"So Javad is letting you go."

She nodded.

"If he's so nice to you, then why are you leaving him? I don't understand any of it. What's this fancy life you're imagining for yourself, can you explain it to me?"

"I'm not looking for anything fancy. I just want to be out of this . . . prison."

"You may as well go away." He suddenly sounded excited. "I can see you'll cause trouble if you're kept around here for too long. You might become a Communist, the way you talk. You might get involved in destructive things." He was a little flushed. "I was afraid of that even before, when you went to that movie studio without telling me, when I discovered a book by Gorky in your room. And now you've gotten it into your head to divorce your husband. You talk about misery in this country. Sohrab never talked like you. He was an obedient boy. But you're going to find out what real inhumanity is when you're there. They put old people away in dungeons, just because they can no longer work and make money. Young people lead lonely, isolated lives. The only thing valued in that country is money. People knife each other on the street for money."

She just listened. This was her father's way of sounding resolute, of not losing his authority over her.

Finally he said, "Do you realize this is going to cost me a lot of money?"

"I don't expect you to—"

"You think you can survive by yourself, a young woman without skills?"

"Thank you. I'm very grateful. I'm sure that will save me a lot of headaches." Her father's sudden generosity moved her. She was about to cry, but she got up and left the room.

The next day Minou filled out the application forms and sent them off. She had to visit the consulate and write to the American Embassy. Now her mind was so focused on the future that the present became blurry. She moved through the days effortlessly. If everything went well she would be able to leave in three months. She planned to stop a day or two in Tehran to visit Farzin before taking off for the United States. Thinking of all this speeded up her days.

One afternoon, while going through her closet and drawers to decide what to take and what to leave behind, she came across her wedding dress (it had developed yellowish stains) and the composition she had written in Javad's class about a woman being bound and sold in a bazaar. Javad's handwriting in red ink was scribbled in the margin. "Symbolic of how things are."

She made a bundle of the dress, the composition, and some other old items and took them into the courtyard. She lit the tin stove Ali used for burning garbage and threw the bundle into it. Flames rose up, making a crackling noise. As she watched the wedding dress become mere ash, she thought of her discomfort in it when she wore it. But then every time she had looked at Javad a wild happiness beat in her chest, singing like a bird. The first time he had kissed her—their breaths combining, her breasts pressing against his chest, her face feeling the roughness of his—she had been lifted and transformed into another being.

How quickly her love for him had diminished. There was something incredible, almost frightening about it. Their lives had been entangled for a brief period and then separated, joltingly.

The flames subsided and she turned to go back inside. A few moments later, alone in her room, a sense of elation came over her as she thought, I'm going on without Javad, I'm not falling into pieces.

"I was like you, a dreamer, when I was your age," her mother said as they walked away from the old train toward the graveyard where her grandmother was buried.

"No harm in trying things." How inadequate that sounded, as though she were talking about choosing a dress.

Minou had obtained a passport and a visa more quickly than she had expected. She could leave now and take an English language course while she waited to hear from colleges. She would be leaving in two days.

They went through a small bazaar. They stopped by a florist and bought a bouquet of flowers to put on the grave.

At the entrance to the graveyard a man was kneeling on the ground, inscribing epitaphs on gravestones. He was old and sad-looking. Not far from him sat another old man selling ceramic pots. He was adding up something on an abacus. Minou paused to look at the pots. She remembered Javad reciting a poem by Omar Khayyám when they had come across the broken masonry in Band Gir.

The graveyard with its dusty, crouching trees was filled with people wailing. Rivulets of dirty water trickled through the yard. Her grandmother's grave had a shiny, black stone. One line, in large letters, was inscribed on it: "She was born good and died good. May her soul rest in heaven."

Several other graves with identical stones stood around it. They belonged to relatives close to her grandmother who had died before her—her two sisters, her husband, a brother, two small children. Inscribed on the stones were the causes of their deaths: typhoid, malaria, appendicitis, heart attack.

She put the flowers on her grandmother's grave. A toad stood near a pile of leaves. It opened its mouth periodically to take in gulps of air.

"She was so nice to you," her mother said. "She kept telling me, 'You can have the boy, but leave Minou to me.'"

A woman's soft voice reached them. "Why did you die, why did you do this to me?" She was kneeling by a raised grave, her black *chador* covering every part of her like a shroud.

Minou imagined her grandmother under the ground, lifeless. She began to cry. Her mother joined in. They wept for a long time.

What would her grandmother have said about her suffering, considering her own endurance of calamities? Minou wondered. She had given birth to four children by a man she had never loved. He had beaten her to make her sleep with him.

She had become widowed when she was only thirty-five years old. Her husband died of appendicitis. The big house they had lived in began to fall apart, its doors infested with termites, the stained-glass windows chipped and cracked, the flower beds choked with weeds, the pool covered by thick green algae.

Then she sold the house and almost everything in it and moved in with Narghes, her oldest daughter. Minou could still vividly recall the day when men came in and took things away from the house—silver dishes, the chandelier with its bright crystal hangings (Minou took some off and held them against the light to see the colors embodied in their transparency), hand-painted vases, silverware with floral patterns, mirrors with gilded frames, velvet clothes. Her grandmother stood in the doorway of a room with her *chador* on. She said, "Let them take them."

She herself had gradually faded, losing weight, her senses becoming dulled. Her skin became specked with liver spots and her gray hair by henna that would not stay on evenly. A taciturn expression came onto her face. She panted heavily and had to sit down to catch her breath.

She had visions of *jinn* staring at her from the depths of sunlight. She threw pails of water on them and shouted, "Get lost." They had been created out of fire (they were the only living things that thrived in hell) and extinguished when immersed in water.

She would not go into the courtyard at night. She was afraid of *divs* that lived in the dark. She had seen their horns and eyes shining in the moonlight. If they saw her they would attack her with their claws and carry her away.

Her talk became incoherent, jumping between the past and the present, mixing up the sequence of events. She told Minou of a nightmare she had. "The *div* sat on my chest. I felt paralyzed. I could not move. I could hardly breathe. When I woke I was sweating all over, a cold sweat." Then she spoke about injuring herself as a child, falling down the stairway of a basement, where her parents kept earthen jars of pickles.

It comforted her to think of joining those she had lost. She talked with the dead, her parents, brothers, sisters, uncles, and aunts, all coming to her one by one or in groups, holding hands somewhere in the sky, smiling at her, beckoning to her to join them.

She said, "Everything seeded in the earth sprouts one day; the sun sets on one side and rises on another. That's how it is with the dead, you bury the dead and the soul is resurrected. We're guests in this world and we will all have to leave it for the real and permanent world beyond. Hopefully we will unite in heaven, a place full of flowers and birds and streams, with gaiety all around."

She made Minou feel she would never lose anyone permanently.

Then she could hardly hear or see. A sickly-sweet smell permeated her room in Narghes' house, where she lay most of the day, a smell of medicine and illness. She had moments of terror then, that she could go to hell after all for sins she had forgotten about—perhaps she had inadvertently looked at a man or missed a few days of fasting for no good reason.

One night she died in her sleep of "old age." Internal bleeding of an organ, heart failure, blood stopped in her arteries?

In the morning, by the time Minou got to Narghes' house, her grandmother had already been taken away. Sunlight fell over the rug in her grandmother's room, but she was no longer there to warm her legs in it. A large golden fly buzzed in the air.

"It's her soul," her uncle said, coming in and seeing
Minou crying.

Minou stared at the fly, terrified that a bit of her grandmother was trapped in it.

She and her mother left the graveyard and went to the
adjacent shrine. They put on the *chadors* they had brought
along. Families had spread blankets in the courtyard of the
shrine and set up samovars and water pipes, picnicking.

By the door of the shrine they took their shoes off and
checked them at a counter. They walked around the
chambers, which glittered with mirrors and candlelight
and silver and gold ornaments. A prayer session was going
on in one room, with women standing in rows, reclining
and rising as the *aghound* said the prayers. In another
chamber an *aghound* was giving a sermon and men and
women had gathered around him, listening, some crying.
In the last chamber people were lighting candles and in-
serting them in a holder.

Her mother lit a candle and said, "This is to bless your
future."

Then they left the shrine. It was getting dark and a few
stars had appeared in the sky. Minou walked alongside her
mother, the sound of all the weeping still in her ears.

25

Months later, in Boston, Minou looked back at that period of her life as if it were a feverish reverie. She had a dream, when she was in bed with the flu, that reminded her of the feeling she had in those months. In the dream she was groping to find her way out of a dim, unfamiliar place. As she got used to the dark she saw thousands of tiny black eyes staring at her. She looked closer. Rows and rows of beetles stood on the walls and ceiling, quite still, as if they had been fighting and were now at truce.

She was going to Boston University and lived in a small apartment near it. The apartment was sparsely furnished with a bed, a bureau, a wooden desk, and two chairs. The kitchen had few utensils, but she was rarely at home anyway. It was easier and not much more expensive to eat at the school's cafeteria. She led an orderly life, mostly studying. Sohrab was in Madison, Wisconsin, and she had spent only a short period of time with him before she came to Boston. Except for a few hand-painted boxes and vases, given to her as farewell presents before she left, her clothes and some books, she had hardly anything with her from home. Once, looking inside a book she had brought with her, she found a pressed fig leaf, perfectly preserved. When she picked it up it crumbled into dust.

Minou had finally gotten a divorce from Javad, through her father. Javad would not be responsible for sending back her dowry, most of which he had left behind in Abadan. And in return, Minou would not have to repay his loan.

Minou liked Boston. Almost every day there were demonstrations and strikes on Boston streets, antinuclear rallies, complaints against low pay for the employees of a restaurant, against bad conditions for the subway workers. On the radio and television there was mockery of a senator or the President. In public toilets, on the walls, outrageous remarks were scribbled. Yet, to Minou, there was something safe and orderly underneath it all. She had a sense that she could say and do what she wanted without danger, and this filled her with a sense of an almost bottomless liberation. It was a little like the dreams she had as a child of floating in the air without any fear of falling, carefree and light.

There was a tranquil beauty to some of the more strictly residential sections where the streets were lined with large frame houses and trees and the air was fragrant with flowers. Ivy dripped down some walls. The soft noises of children, television, lawnmowers, and sprinklers gently splashing water on the green lawns rose from the backyards. Only occasionally someone went by, pushing a baby carriage or walking a dog with brushed, clean hair.

How different this all was from Abadan and Ahvāz. The Kārūn River, oil streaking into its waters, the nasal, mournful singing of the Arab boat owners. Those remorselessly hot and stagnant days. The lurid light, the jagged black shadows of palm trees. That dismal Square in Abadan with its scraggly trees and food stalls and its partly unpaved ground from which dust rose like vapor. Menace always in the air.

Here her days went as she planned, orderly and predictable. Human interaction seemed simplified. She immersed herself in a quiet routine like a person convalescing from an illness.

On a Sunday morning Minou was sitting in her apartment, reading the *Tehran Tribune,* a Persian-language biweekly paper published in the United States, oriented toward Iranians. Her eyes caught Javad Partovi's name in the first line of an article.

Javad Partovi and Pari Soleimani were arrested in Tehran on Friday, March 3, 1978, on a charge of publishing certain articles critical of the government in *Bidar,* the newspaper they coedited. They have each been sentenced to three years in jail. Partovi had said to the policemen arresting him, "I want to be a living man and that embodies expressing what I think is the truth. I am not willing to go on as a shadow, a mere phantom of a person...."

So Javad and Pari's relationship had endured. A flurry of emotions brought tears to Minou's eyes. He had taken a risk of the sort he had tried to avoid when he was in Abadan. Had his alliance with Pari given him more strength, or was this a desperate act, a sign of deeper dissatisfaction?

She wondered if Karim had a part in their arrest. She had read that Bandeh Khoda's activities had spread, gained significance on the national level.

A little later, Minou was standing by the Charles River, watching the boats moving on the surface of the water. Men and women, mostly students, passed by or sat on the grass, their voices mixing with the noise of the traffic. It was near dusk and the sun kept going in and out of clouds. She was startled as a boat approached the bank to see—could she really believe it?—that one of the passengers was Javad, with his black, wavy hair and stooping posture, and the other Pari, with her oblong profile. She had on a tight-fitting dress and high heels. He did the rowing while she held on to the sides of the boat, and kept looking at his face. He turned to her, and Minou thought she detected a smile on his face. The boat came closer. Now Minou could see that the woman's hair had reddish highlights and the man's hair, far from being black, was darkish blond. The man beached the boat. Then he held the woman's hand and helped her out. The two of them laughed as the woman almost fell and then straightened up.

The vision of Javad and Pari together had evoked no pain, she realized—she was free within herself and of him—but she was aware of another ache, for her country that went on breathing, living in her.

It was 1981. Minou was back in Iran for a brief visit. Now she stood on the wharf in Abadan. Pieces of wrecked ships, rusted chains, and metal repair instruments, stacks of empty crates covered by moss were scattered on the shore. There was nothing remaining of the fishermen's huts that used to stand there. The water, black with petroleum seeping in from shattered pipelines, was stagnant and tepid, not like a flowing river.

Since she left here six years before, a lot had happened. There had been a change of government, the Shah overthrown. A war with Iraq had demolished much of Abadan and Ahvāz. Iraq wanted, among other things, to regain the Shatt-al-Arab waterway to the Persian Gulf. The war was at an impasse, making it possible for her to visit, but Iranian soldiers stood everywhere in town, waiting for the fighting to begin again.

Whole streets had vanished, with blocks of houses and buildings torn away (a little earlier she had gone to the house where she and Javad lived and found in its place a heap of stones and rubbish). There were few residents left in the town. Hundreds of people had been maimed and killed, others had fled. Riding in from the airport (she arrived on the single nonmilitary flight that came into Abadan once a week and left the same day), she had a false impression that nothing had changed. She had looked out on the same arid brown roads with a low chain of hills in the distance, the unexpected bright patches of wildflowers glistening in the sunshine.

Minou suddenly heard footsteps. Then she saw two Iranian soldiers, holding the arms of a woman, approaching from behind a partially wrecked ship.

"Please let me go, have mercy on me," the woman begged.

"It's God's will for sinners to be punished."

"They're going to kill me."

"You shouldn't have been sinful."

"Have mercy on me," she repeated in a piercing voice. "Let me go. I will live somewhere quietly."

"Why didn't you think of that before?"

She started to weep. One of the soldiers slapped her. She began to whimper like a child.

Minou had a close look at her before they all turned away from the wharf and went into the avenue. Her eyebrows were plucked very thin and she had heavy mascara on her eyelashes. Two of her front teeth were gold, two others black with decay. Minou had read that prostitutes were being arrested in Abadan and some executed. It was here that she used to come with Ali in the evenings, where she had seen prostitutes waiting for soldiers to get off the ships. The terror of some of the incidents she had lived through in Abadan came pouring back to her. She wondered what had become of Javad. He could be still in jail. He could be living somewhere with Pari. She thought of the fire in the cinema and all the talk that Abadan was going to burn up one day.

The sunset came on suddenly, the same vivid sunset that she used to watch from a window. She left the wharf, walking toward the avenue. The driver of the car she had rented would come there shortly to take her back to the airport. The streetlights were not turned on even though it was getting dark. Probably there was a blackout because of the war. Some of the bulbs were smashed anyway. There were dark shadows everywhere. Rubbish was being swept up by a team of men. On the wall, next to a heap of rubble, was written in blood: "These are drops of our blood, spilled for our country."

A full moon came out. Soon stars, those incredibly bright stars that dripped like silver water, would appear. A truck carrying Iranian soldiers passed by, sending whiffs of dust into the air. The soldiers smiled and waved at her, cheerful and excited about something. She waved back. (All day she had been afraid a soldier would come over to her and search her.) Other soldiers came to the street and began to set up tents and mosquito nets. Some of them washed their hands and faces in a narrow stream, getting ready for prayers.

A bomb could fall on them unexpectedly. If that happened they would think they were dying as God-fearing people. As for her, there was no such comfort.